Dedicated to Saint Jude
and to my wonderful family for
their unending love and support

Acknowledgements

I would like to thank Michelle Stafford and Tiffany Scott for being among the first readers and generously providing helpful edits and reviews. Your encouraging support has meant a lot to me.

The Haunting
on
Raventree Lane

Elizabeth Shumka

The Haunting on Raventree Lane

Copyright © 2016 Elizabeth Shumka

Author's note: This novel is a work of fiction. Names, characters, business establishments, and incidences are either products of the author's imagination or used fictitiously. All characters are fictional, and any similarity to people living or dead is purely coincidental.

Edited by Christine Shumka

Photographs by Anastasia Shumka

ISBN-13: 978-1539795308
ISBN-10: 1539795306

Chapter 1

It was late at night when I opened the front door of the house. I hesitantly walked inside. I tried to be quiet, but the old floor boards creaked beneath my feet. There were no lights on, and it took me a moment to adjust to the darkness. There was a carved spiral staircase that led to the second floor. I realized this was not the farmhouse that my mom and I lived in, and I was confused as to why I was there. I tried to turn and run, but the front door slammed behind me and locked. Paralyzing fear gripped me as I tried in vain to get the door open. I was trapped. I could hear a door open upstairs and the sound of footsteps approaching the top of the stairs. I looked for a place to hide and quickly crouched behind a marble pillar in the ornate entry way. I wrapped my arms around myself as I shivered in fear. An older man appeared at the top of the stairs. He didn't seem to see me as he made his way down. Suddenly, he gasped as he was forcibly propelled forward down the stairs. He tried to grab onto the hand rail, but it was too late. I watched in horror as his arms and legs flailed wildly before he landed in a crumpled pile at the bottom of the stairs. I ran out from my hiding place from behind the pillar. In that moment, I was more concerned about the old man than I was for myself.

"Are you OK?" I asked in a panicked voice. "I'll go get help." Before I could go, he reached up and grabbed my hand. It was ice cold, and he looked at me pleadingly with his dark brown eyes.

"Run," he begged. "Run as fast as you can, and never come back. There's danger here for you." His limp hand fell away from mine as he took his last breath. I heard a sound at the top of the stairs. I looked up and saw a young girl about seven or eight with blond hair and blue eyes clutching a doll.

"Hurry, we need to get help. Call 911," I yelled up at her.

She just stood there as an evil smile spread across her face. A wicked laugh escaped from her mouth and echoed through the cavernous entry way. I coiled back in horror at the malevolent sound coming from the girl. She raised her hand up and pointed at me. "You're next, Lauren."

"Lauren, Lauren, Lauren," the voice kept getting louder. I woke with a start. It was my mom calling me from downstairs. It took me a moment to realize that I was back in my bedroom. It was just a bad dream.

"Lauren, hurry up. Your breakfast is getting cold."

"I'll be down in a second," I yelled back. My heart was still racing as I pulled on a pair of jeans and a shirt and made my way down to the kitchen table. There was a plate filled with an omelet and toast. I grabbed a piece of toast and took a bite.

"You looked flushed," Mom said as she brushed a lock of blond hair out of my eyes. "Are you feeling OK?"

"I had a bad dream," I replied in between mouthfuls of toast.

"You'll have to tell me about it after work. I'm running late," she said as she glanced at her watch. "Oh, and after you finish your chores, don't forget to organize your school supplies. School starts in a few days."

"I know," I replied despondently. It was the end of summer, and although I did well in school, I didn't look forward to going back.

"I'll be home around six tonight. Call me if you need anything." I barely looked up as she headed out the front door. Mom worked long hours at the library trying to make ends meet since my dad had died when I was three years old. I was twelve now and old enough to be alone and help out with chores around our farm in Montana. Mr. Williams and his son farmed the land for us, and they would check in on me from time to time. I hurried to finish breakfast so that I could go outside and enjoy the last few days of freedom.

Chapter 2

I walked outside the farmhouse and headed toward the barn. It was a beautiful day. As I glanced out at the fields, I could see short stumps of grain stalks left over from harvesting. Stubble covered the ground, and I missed the tall golden wheat that used to blanket the fields. There were a few stray clouds in the sky, and I closed my eyes as I soaked in the warmth of the sun from the last few days of summer. I finally headed over to the barn to take care of my horse Susie. She whinnied softly when she saw me coming. I told her about my bad dream as I cleaned out the stall and brushed her white coat. She nudged me as if reminding me that I had forgotten about her cup of oats.

"I didn't forget," I said as I headed into the barn. There was a small tack room off to the side of the barn where the oats were stored. It was a dark windowless room filled with old farm equipment, saddles, and other odds and ends. It was dark and dusty, and I always tried to spend the least amount of time in there. I propped open the door, and I was about to go in when I thought I heard someone walking around the barn. I stepped outside.

"Hello, is someone there?" I called out. A stray cloud went across the sun casting a shadow on the barn. No one answered except for the slight breeze that made an eerie sound as it passed through the breezeway. A sudden chill filled the air, and I felt fearful as I peered into the pitch black tack room. I just had to run in and scoop out a cup of oats and run out. I had done it a million times before. I took a few steps in, and as I reached into the bag of oats, I heard the sound of footsteps again.

I turned to see who was there, but I only saw a flash of white before the door slammed shut and I was engulfed in complete blackness. I tried not to panic. It was just the wind, I told myself as I made my way to the door. I found the handle and pushed, but the door seemed to be jammed from the outside. I pushed harder, but it wouldn't budge. Sweat started to roll down my forehead. I took a step backwards, and a spider web caught in my hair. I screamed and hopped up and down as I tried to get the spider web out of my hair. Something scurried by my feet, probably a mouse. I ran toward the door and banged loudly on it.

"Help me. Someone help me," I screamed. Footsteps sounded outside the door. "Please help me. I'm locked inside," I begged. I waited in silence, hoping to hear if someone was trying to open the door. Instead what I heard horrified me. It sounded like a child's laughter, only it was a sinister laugh filled with such malevolence and evil that I stepped back from the door. I was more afraid of what was waiting outside the door than I was of the spiders and mice inside the room with me. It reminded me of my nightmare from last night, and I became filled with terror. The laughter died down outside, and an icy chill began to permeate the room. I shivered as I heard something moving in the corner. It was too big to be a mouse. I turned to see what it was, but it was too dark inside to see anything. That's when I heard it again. The diabolic laughter, only this time it was coming from inside the room. I rushed to the door and banged as hard as I could as I screamed for help. Tears were pouring down my face as I begged someone to help. The laughter was coming closer. It was too late. Suddenly, the door opened, and I stumbled out.

"Are you all right, Lauren?" Mom asked. "What happened?"

"Something evil locked me in there," I sobbed. I babbled incoherently for a few minutes about a child and wicked laughter. It took me a few minutes to realize that Mom was home from work in the middle of the day.

"How come you're home so early?" I asked as I brushed a few stray tears from my face.

"Something happened to Grandma," she said.

"Did Grandma get arrested again?" The last time Mom had gone to help Grandma, she had gotten arrested for running a high stakes bingo game out of her retirement home. The charges were eventually dropped, but she was banned from the retirement home.

"No. Grandma hasn't been arrested. She broke her arm," Mom replied vaguely.

"How did she break her arm?" I asked suspiciously.

Mom sighed. "She was at the race track, and she was so excited when she won that she fell down the stairs and broke her arm." Grandma was not your normal milk and cookies kind of grandma. When most kids were little, they played Go Fish or Old Maid with their grandparents. Instead Grandma taught me how to play poker and blackjack. We only played with jelly beans, but I was sure that she was cheating at cards and stealing my candy whenever I wasn't looking.

"I got a flight out to California tomorrow. I'll get back as soon as I can."

"Can I go with you?" I begged.

"No, school starts in two days. You'll be staying with your Aunt Rose."

"No, not Aunt Rose," I exclaimed in horror. She wasn't even my aunt. Mom and Rose grew up together, and Mom had always considered her family. "Can I stay with John?" John lived on the farm next to ours. He was like an older brother to me and my best friend.

"John lives in a small house with his parents. There wouldn't be any room for you."

"How about Miss Peters, can I stay with her?" I begged.

"Gladys is working extra shifts at the library for me. Besides, she lives too far away from your school. Rose lives just a few blocks away. You can walk to school and back home every day. You'll have a great time. You'll see. Besides, I won't be gone very long." I knew I had lost the argument, and I resigned myself to the fact that I was staying with Aunt Rose.

"Can I take Susie out for one last ride?"

"As long as you're home for dinner and you finish packing tonight. We have to leave first thing in the morning so that I can make my afternoon flight."

"OK," I replied as Mom retreated back into the farmhouse to get ready for her trip.

Chapter 3

I headed out to the barn and put a bridle and saddle on Susie. Thankfully, I had left the saddle in an empty stall so I didn't have to go back into the tack room. I rode along the river toward John's house. I had a lot to tell him. As I rode up to his house, John's dog Moose came bounding out the screen door toward me. He spooked Susie, and she sidestepped a bit before I could calm her down. I got off and tied her to a fence post. The big, black German Shepherd jumped on my shoulders and licked my face. "I missed you too," I said as I hugged him back.

John finally made his way outside to see what all the commotion was about. Although he was only a year older than me, he was very tall and lanky. His brown hair had been recently trimmed, and his skin was tan from being outside in the sun all summer.

He had bright blue eyes, and all the girls at school seemed to be in love with him. I never really understood why.

"Please tell me you didn't bring another ridiculous outfit to dress up my dog in," John exclaimed.

"Too late," I said as I stepped back from Moose. Moose stood perfectly still with a serious expression on his face and enormous bunny ears on his head. I giggled, and even John couldn't hide his smile.

"You're going to make a sissy out of him."

"He loves it," I replied as I took off the bunny ears and picked up one of his tennis balls and threw it into a field. Moose happily bounded after it. I sat down on the grass in a field that overlooked the river. "I have so much to tell you," I said with anticipation. John sat down next to me. He would never admit it, but he liked to gossip as much as I did.

"I had this terrible dream that there was this evil girl that pushed an old man down the stairs and killed him. Then she laughed and told me that I was next."

"That's a terrible dream," John admitted.

"It gets worse. I went to get some oats for Susie, and someone locked me in the tack room. I heard the same evil laughter that I heard in my dream. Thankfully, Mom was there to let me out."

"Did you see who locked you in the barn?"

"No, I just heard someone walking around. Do you think it might have been the same girl from my nightmare?" I asked.

"But she was just in your dream, and you didn't see who locked you inside," John reasoned.

"That's true."

"It could have been someone else or the wind knocking the door shut."

"I guess so." Now that I thought about it, John was right. It was probably nothing. It was actually better to think that it was just the wind than some evil demon child that was plotting to kill me. John always made me feel better. "Something else happened."

"What?" John asked.

"Grandma broke her arm, and Mom's flying to California tomorrow to take care of her. Guess who I have to stay with?"

"Miss Peters?" John guessed.

"No. Aunt Rose."

John's eyes grew large. "Not Rowdy Rose?" he exclaimed. Rose had gotten the nickname Rowdy

Rose when she was a little girl. She was an only child and a spoiled brat that was used to getting her way. She was ill-tempered and had a short fuse. She was known around town for picking fights and offending pretty much everybody. Since she was built like a football player, most people let her have her way. "I'm so sorry. Maybe I can ask my parents if you can stay with us," John replied as he looked down on me with pity.

"I already asked my mom, and she said that there wasn't any room at your house, but thanks anyways." I looked down at my watch. It was close to dinner time. "I should get going."

"I'll see you at school on Monday," John said as he waved goodbye and went back into the house. I hurried to untie Susie and head home. We half trotted and half galloped the rest of the way home. I took off Susie's saddle and bridle and let her out into the pasture. As I walked up to the house, I could smell the most wonderful aroma permeating the air.

"Hurry up and wash your hands. Dinner is ready. I tried to use up everything that would spoil in the refrigerator since we won't be here."

"Wow, this looks delicious." The table was filled with biscuits and gravy, roasted chicken, creamed corn, and blueberry pie. I hurriedly washed my hands and sat down. Mom said a quick prayer of grace before I filled my plate with the heavenly goodness. We ate in silence as I reached for seconds and thirds. I had to unzip my pants before I could I eat my slice of blueberry pie. This almost made up for the bad nightmare and being locked in the tack room. I sat back in pure bliss and closed my eyes.

"You better go upstairs and pack before you fall asleep."

"Thanks for an awesome meal, Mom."

"You're welcome," she said as she smiled. It always made her happy that I loved her food. I got up from the table and went upstairs to my bedroom. I turned on the light, and it filled the room with a warm glow. I loved the faded flower wall paper and the lace curtains. I was going to miss being away from here. I pulled out an old suitcase and piled everything from my dresser drawers and closet into it. I didn't have a lot of clothes. I put my bag filled with my school supplies next to my suitcase so that I wouldn't forget it. I brushed my teeth and put on my pajamas. Mom stepped briefly into my bedroom to kiss me goodnight. I opened the book that I was reading about vampires and fell asleep with the lights on.

I was disoriented when I woke up. It was dark, and I was no longer in my bedroom. I was in a long hallway with doors on either side. Candles flickered on the walls, and haunting music floated upwards from an organ being played from downstairs. I had to find a way out. There was a maze of hallways, and every time I turned down one, there were several more to choose from. I went around a corner and was startled to see a disfigured girl standing in front of me. Her head was caved in, and her face was filled with terror. I was about to scream until I realized that it was a just mirror that had distorted my own image into something grotesque. It took me a moment to pull myself together. I was lost in a haunted house, and the only thing that I knew was that I had to get out.

I decided to follow the sound of the organ music since it was coming from the floor below and the front door would have to be nearby. I made my way down another hallway, and I could hear the music getting louder. I could see a banister and an ornate spiral staircase leading downstairs. It was the same staircase from my dream the night before. I was afraid to go down it. I cautiously peered over the banister to the floor below. I could see an older woman wearing a long gray dress playing the organ. Her white hair was piled haphazardly on top of her head. Her fingers moved across the keys in a demented manner. She stopped suddenly and looked up at me, her crazed eyes locking with mine.

"You must leave now. Hurry," she said as she motioned for me to come down. "Run as fast as you can and never come back. There's danger here for you." She turned back around and dramatically raised her hands above the organ. Then she violently pushed down on all the keys at once, making a deafening sound.

I stumbled backwards into the shadows and knocked something to the ground as I tried to cover my ears. The loud sound stopped suddenly. I sat up abruptly and realized that I was back in my bedroom. Sunlight poured in through the curtains, and I could see the mangled contents of my alarm clock on the floor. I must have knocked it off my dresser when it went off. It was just a dream. A sense of relief washed over me.

Chapter 4

"Lauren, hurry up. We have to leave soon," Mom called from downstairs. I had overslept, and I hurried to get dressed. I rushed down to the kitchen table and started eating the oatmeal Mom had made for me.

"You look tired. Did you get enough sleep?" Mom asked as she felt my forehead.

"I'm fine. I just had a bad dream," I said in between mouthfuls of oatmeal.

"Again? It must be those vampire books that you're reading."

"They're love stories," I protested.

"About vampires?" she questioned. Mom and I did not have the same taste in books. "Well, hurry up and get your chores done so that we can leave."

"OK," I said gloomily. I went outside to feed the chickens and gather eggs. I gave them extra mealworms today as a treat. I was going to miss them. Even Big Bertha the Barred Rock hen who pecked my bottom every time I bent down to collect eggs. I walked over to the barn and cleaned out the stall. I fed Susie some apples and carrots that I had brought over from the house. I didn't want to admit that I was too afraid to go back into the tack room to get her oats. She seemed content with the apple. "Don't worry. I'll be back soon," I told Susie as I brushed her coat out. I could hear Mom calling from the house, and I reluctantly went inside.

"Lauren, hurry up and help me load the car." I ran upstairs to get my suitcase and school supplies. As Mom pulled out of the driveway, I longing looked at Susie grazing in the field. "Don't worry about the animals. Mr. Williams will take good care of them," she reassured me.

We rode in silence on the way over to Aunt Rose's house. She was a real estate agent who lived in a small bungalow in town. Mom mumbled something about how much fun Aunt Rose and I were going to have, but she didn't sound very convincing, and I stopped listening after a while. We turned down a street named Raventree Lane in the historic part of Bozeman and pulled into the driveway of a towering three story brick mansion. It looked dark and imposing.

"Where are we?" I asked.

"I just told you. Aunt Rose was the real estate agent that got this listing, but she thought it was such a great deal that she bought it for herself. It's still just a few blocks from your school. Isn't it beautiful?"

I wasn't sure if beautiful was the word that I would use. Scary and ominous would better describe it. I stepped out of the car and got my suitcase and bags. I looked up at the three story monstrosity. Although it was a bright summer day, the house looked dark and uninviting. I peered up and thought I saw a curtain being drawn back from a third story window. Someone was watching us. A chill ran down my spine.

"Do you think it's haunted?" I asked.

"Lauren, please don't make this any harder than it already is." The stress of Grandma's accident was starting to take a toll on Mom, and she looked like she was on the verge of tears. I felt bad for upsetting her. The front door opened suddenly, and Aunt Rose appeared. She wore pointy glasses with rhinestones, and her frizzy strawberry blond hair waved wildly around her face. Aunt Rose was in her thirties, and although she was built like a lumberjack, she was wearing a flowing, floral dress and the most beautiful bejeweled sandals that I had ever seen.

"I love your shoes, Aunt Rose."

"I have fifty more pairs up in my bedroom. You can try them on any time that you want."

"Really? Thank you," I said excitedly. Mom smiled. She looked happy that we were getting along. Maybe this wasn't going to be as bad as I thought. Rose ushered us through the front door. My joy was short lived the moment that I stepped inside the house. The grand foyer had a marble column and ornate spiral staircase. It was the exact same staircase from my nightmare. My heart sunk as I stood there in shock. This couldn't be happening.

"Over here is an organ that was built into the house. I'm not sure if it works," Aunt Rose commented. This just kept getting worse and worse.

"Hurry up, Lauren. Aunt Rose is giving us a tour." I dropped my suitcase and ran to catch up. I didn't want to be alone. There was a formal parlor off to the side with a few pieces of antique furniture. Another doorway led into a grand dining room with a long table and a large chandelier. It was quite impressive. Next to the dining room was a smaller but updated kitchen. A small toy poodle mix was sleeping on a bed in the corner.

"Hi, Poopsie," I said as I reached down to pet her. She bared her yellowed rotted teeth at me and growled. I backed away quickly.

"What's wrong, Poopsie? Did Lauren say something to upset my precious little princess?" Aunt Rose asked as she scooped the mangy little dog into her arms. Poopsie glared back at me. Long, stringy, saliva stained hair hung from her chin. I was pretty sure that she was called Poopsie since she still pooped inside the house and you had to watch where you stepped. "Let's go upstairs, and I'll show you your bedroom," Aunt Rose said as she put the dog back on her bed.

I looked up at the top of the spiral staircase expecting to see the little girl from my nightmare, but she wasn't there. I grabbed my mom's hand as we walked up the stairs just to be on the safe side. Aunt Rose showed us two large guest bedrooms and a bathroom before she showed me my bedroom.

"Isn't it perfect for a little girl?" Rose exclaimed. The walls were covered in pink floral wallpaper, and there was a large pink canopy bed in the center of the room. A huge dollhouse and antique rocking chair were tucked into the corner. It should have been every little girl's dream, but there was something wrong with the room. It was ice cold. There was a large dead tree outside the window that blocked any sunlight from coming in, and a black raven perching on one of the branches started making a bloodcurdling sound. I hurriedly stepped back out.

"Did a little girl used to live here?" I asked.

"I'm sure many children have lived in this house since it was built in 1880," Aunt Rose replied. "Let me show you my bedroom." It was a large room with an intricately carved bed. There were shoes and clothes scattered everywhere.

"This is such an amazing house. Now we just have to find you the perfect husband," Mom said. "Is there anyone special?" Mom believed in true love and wanted everyone to find it.

"I just signed up on a dating website, and I'm hopeful that I'll meet someone."

"You're so wonderful. I'm sure that you'll find someone very soon." Mom always saw the good in people even if it wasn't there. "I should get going so that I don't miss my plane." We all walked out to the car to say goodbye. Mom held me close for the longest time. "I'm going to miss you so much, Pumpkin."

I was about to tell Mom that this was the house from my nightmares and that she had to get me out of there, but when I looked up, I could see that she was crying. "I'm going to miss you too," I said instead. It was too late to do anything anyways. I cried as I watched her car drive away.

"Stop crying," Aunt Rose barked at me as she ushered me inside. "Go put your things away. Dinner will be ready soon." I grabbed my suitcase and bags and ran up the stairs. I cautiously peered into the room to make sure that no one was in there. It looked empty, and I quickly threw my things into the closet and ran as fast as I could downstairs.

"That was fast, Little Quack Quack," Aunt Rose said as she stirred something on the stove. I had forgotten how much I hated that nickname. When I was three, Aunt Rose asked me what I wanted to be when I grew up. I said a duck. I loved ducks and was too young to realize that you couldn't grow up to be a duck. Aunt Rose called me Little Quack Quack ever since, and I had grown to hate it. "Go set the kitchen table."

"OK," I said as Aunt Rose directed me to where all the plates and silverware were located. We sat down, and she spooned orange goop onto my plate.

"It's macaroni and cheese. Doesn't it look good?" Aunt Rose proclaimed proudly. I love macaroni and cheese, but I had never seen it look like this. Aunt Rose took a bite. "Why aren't you eating?"

"We're supposed to say grace before meals," I said with my hands folded in prayer. Aunt Rose had a guilty look on her face.

"Oh, that's right. Um, good bread, good meat, good God, let's eat." I had never heard grace said that way, but I guess it counted. I took my first bite and nearly cracked my tooth. Half the macaroni had not been cooked all the way through.

"Good, isn't it?" I tried to nod and smile and then spit the offensive food into a napkin when Aunt Rose wasn't looking. I could forgive Aunt Rose for being rude and living in a haunted house, but serving inedible food was criminal.

"I think I'll go to bed now," I said before Aunt Rose could spoon another serving onto my plate.

"Good idea. School starts tomorrow."

"I know," I groaned.

"Good night, Little Quack Quack."

"Good night." I cautiously climbed the stairs and walked toward the bedroom. It was dark, and I regretted not keeping a light on when I was there earlier. I stood in the doorway for a moment. The moonlight filtered through the dead branches outside the bedroom window casting eerie shadows across the room. I hesitantly reached inside the room to turn on the light. There was a bloodcurdling scream the moment the lights flickered on, and two black eyes stared back at me through the window. I stumbled backwards as I saw a raven flap its wings wildly and fly away. It was just a bird, I told myself. We had probably scared each other. I quickly closed the drapes and got ready for bed. The room was ice cold, and I pulled the covers all the way up to my chin. I thought about reading my vampire book but decided against it, just in case it was giving me nightmares. I planned on keeping the light on all night since nothing bad ever happened with the lights on. I was exhausted and fell asleep shortly after I got into bed.

Elizabeth Shumka

A loud noise shook my bed and woke me up. I sat up and was disoriented for a moment. The light was still on, and I realized that I was in the large pink canopy bed in Aunt Rose's house. It was just a thunderstorm. Rain pelleted the window, and I could see flashes of lightning through a gap in the curtains. It was followed by a violent thunderous sound that shook the whole house. My room was so cold now that I could see my breath in front of me. I shivered in my bed. I was about to run to my Aunt's bedroom when the lights flickered and went out, plunging the room into complete darkness. I could hear the creaking of my closet door as it slowly opened. I became paralyzed with fear, unable to move. It was too dark to see anything, but I could hear something moving under my bed.

"Poopsie, is that you?" I asked with a shaky voice. Maybe the storm had scared her and she was hiding under my bed. "Poopsie?" There was more scratching under my bed. I was afraid that the dog was frightened or hurt, and I got up the courage to check under the bed. I slowly put one foot on the ground. The scratching under the bed stopped, and all I could hear was the sound of the rain outside. I cautiously put my other foot on the floor and slowly got down on my hands and knees to peer under the bed. "Poopsie?" It was pitch black, and it was difficult to see anything, but I thought I saw the outline of something dark. A flash of lightning lit up the room for a second, and I could see the glint of a knife under the bed. A small blond girl with glowing red eyes stared back at me. An evil smile spread across her face as she reached forward and grabbed my arm. She was surprisingly strong and started to pull me under the bed with her. I didn't have time to scream as I pulled back as hard as I could. Her face was close to mine as heard her say, "Where's my mommy?" I pushed against the bed with my free hand, and I got enough leverage to break free. As I fell backwards, I could see her start to crawl out from under the bed towards me with a knife in her hand. I scrambled to get up and run. I felt a cut to the back of my leg as stood up, but I just kept running forward out of the room. I turned down the hallway and put my hand against the wall to guide my way as I ran until I found the doorway to my Aunt's bedroom. I burst into the room, screaming hysterically.

"Help me. There's someone under my bed," I cried.

"What? What's wrong?" Aunt Rose said groggily.

"There's an evil girl under my bed, and she tried to kill me," I exclaimed.

"There's nothing under your bed. Go back to sleep," Aunt Rose said angrily.

"Can you at least check?" I begged.

"All right." Aunt Rose reached for her bedside lamp, but it wouldn't turn on. "The storm must have knocked out the electricity."

"Can I at least sleep with you tonight? My mom always let me sleep with her."

"Your mother spoils you rotten."

I tried not to let her comment hurt me, but it did. "Please, just this one night." Another clap of thunder shook the house, and I jumped into her bed.

Aunt Rose finally relented. "All right, but just this once." She rolled over, taking most of the covers with her. I heard her snoring a few minutes later. I pulled the thin sheet over my body and cried myself to sleep.

Chapter 5

"Lauren, hurry up. You're going to be late for school," my aunt called from downstairs. I quickly went to my bedroom to get my clothes. The room didn't look as scary during the day. I tried to tell myself that it was just another bad dream. I felt a sharp pain on the back of my leg as I started to pull on my jeans. As I turned to look, I could see a three inch gash across the back of my calf. I threw on the rest of my clothes, grabbed my backpack, and ran downstairs.

"There's cereal in the cabinet," Aunt Rose said as she sat at the table drinking a cup of coffee. I found a box of cereal that advertised that it was good for weight loss. I guess if Aunt Rose was on a diet, I would be forced to be on one too. I poured what looked like bird seed into a bowl and added milk and sugar to make it palatable.

"You better leave soon or you're going to be late."

"Do you know where my lunch is?" I asked Aunt Rose.

"Don't you get lunch at school?"

"I only get hot lunch on Fridays."

"OK. Let me see what I can find." Aunt Rose grabbed a lunch bag and stuffed something into it. "Here you go. Have a great day, Little Quack Quack." I walked out the front door and headed toward school. A neighbor was outside sweeping the walkway. She looked startled when she saw me.

"You look so much like her," the older woman blurted out.

"Who do I look like?" I asked.

"The little girl that used to live there."

"Who was she?" Before she could answer, two crows landed on a tree nearby and began screeching loudly. The older woman looked up at the house, and all the color drained from her face. I looked up to see what she was looking at, and I could see that the curtain had been pulled back from the third story window. Someone was watching us.

"I've said too much already," the older woman said as she hurried back into her house and locked the door. A chill ran down my spine as I tightened the grip on my backpack and started to run down the street toward my school. I got there in record time. It was the first time that I was actually happy to be there.

The school was a large, two-story building with tall windows on every side. There were very few students there this early in the morning, and I was nervous as I went up the stairs. I saw John walking in the hallway. He was thirteen and in the grade above me. We didn't hang out together at school, but he was always there if I needed him. I flashed him the peace sign. It was our secret signal that I needed to talk and to meet in our secret spot during lunch time. He nodded his head that he understood. I found my classroom and sat down at a desk by the window.

"Did you forget to comb your hair today, Lauren?" a boy in my class named Tommy Carson snickered as he sat in the desk behind me. I had forgotten to brush my hair. I decided to ignore him. I wasn't very popular in school. Other kids thought that I was weird. Maybe it was because I heard and saw things that no else did.

A woman in her thirties with long blond hair entered the classroom. She was petite with sorrowful brown eyes that didn't match the smile on her face. "I'm Miss Sullivan. I'll be your teacher this year." She asked each of us to introduce ourselves and tell everyone what they did this summer. I decided not to say that I was haunted by a ghost and that John and I had solved the mystery behind her death. Instead I said that I went horseback riding and played in the creek. Once the introductions were done, Miss Sullivan had us take out our history books and started our first lesson. She then went on to teach math. I could barely keep my eyes open before the bell finally rang for lunch.

I got my lunch out of my locker and walked to the back of the school where there was a small table behind the school library that no one ever used. John was already there waiting for me. I breathed a sigh of relief as I sat down beside him.

"Who's your teacher this year?" John asked.

"Miss Sullivan," I replied.

"She was my teacher last year. I really like her. She's nice."

"Who's your teacher?" I asked as I opened my lunch bag to see what my aunt had packed for me. I pulled out two diet protein bars.

"Mr. Bartholomew is my teacher. He's new at the school. What is that?" John asked as he pointed to my protein bar. I unwrapped one and took a bite.

I nearly choked. "I think it's sawdust mixed with dirt and fake chocolate chips." He took pity on me and handed me half his ham sandwich.

"We can share."

"Thanks, John."

We both took a few bites of the sandwich before John finally asked. "So what's wrong?"

"Oh, it was so horrifying last night. The lights in my bedroom went out in the storm, and I thought I heard something under my bed. I was worried that it might be my aunt's poodle hiding there because she was hurt or frightened. I decided to check under the bed, and I saw a little blond girl hiding there.

Her eyes were glowing, and she was holding a knife. She grabbed my arm and said, 'Where's my mommy?' and then tried to drag me under the bed."

"Oh my gosh! What did you do?"

"I pulled back as hard as I could and fell backwards. I saw her crawl out from under the bed toward me, and I got up to run. She cut the back of my leg before I could get out of the room." I pulled up my pant leg to show him the cut.

"Then what happened?" John seemed truly intrigued.

"I ran to my aunt's room and begged her to let me sleep with her."

"Did you see the girl again?"

"No, thank goodness. Who do you think she is?"

"Maybe someone murdered her and buried her body in the backyard and now she wants revenge."

"Then why did she say, 'Where's my mommy?'"

"Maybe someone murdered her mother and buried her body in the backyard and now the little girl is looking for her." In either of John's scenarios, there was a body buried in the backyard.

"I don't want to dig up the backyard looking for dead bodies," I adamantly replied.

"OK." John sounded disappointed. "How about if we just find out who the little girl was and then maybe we can figure out why she's there. Did your aunt know anything about a girl who used to live there?"

"I asked her, and she said that a lot of children have probably lived there since the house was built. I did see a neighbor this morning. She said I looked a lot like the little girl that used to live there. I asked her who the little girl was, but the lady seemed frightened and ran back inside her house."

"If the girl lived there in the last fifty years, then Mrs. Harrison would know who she was. She's lived in town forever, and she knows everyone. I could ask my mom if I could go over to your house tomorrow after school. We can stop by Mrs. Harrison's house on the way home."

"Thanks, John. I really appreciate all your help."

The bell rang to come inside, and we both went back to our classrooms. Miss Sullivan had us take out our science books and gave a lecture about different ecosystems. She then had us read silently out of our English books. I hadn't slept well the night before, and I could barely keep my eyes open. I heard a light tapping on the window beside me. I turned to look, and I could see a raven perched on the windowsill outside, staring back at me. Its black eyes focused intently on me. The sky seemed to darken and a chill began to fill the classroom. Fear began to bubble up inside me, but as much as I wanted to, I couldn't look away from the raven. It made an ear piercing scream and flew away suddenly as if something had startled it. I saw a flash of white at the edge of the sill, and as I looked closer, I could see blond hair and two glowing red eyes staring back at me. Only the top part of the child's face was visible, and I couldn't hear the words that she was saying. Suddenly, she lifted up her arm to knock on the window, and I could see the glint of a knife in her hand. I jumped out of my desk and screamed. The entire class stared at me.

"Is everything all right, Lauren?" Miss Sullivan asked, concerned.

I looked back at the window, and there was nothing there. I wasn't even sure if I had fallen asleep and dreamt it. "There was a spider," I said lamely. The kids in my class laughed at me, and my face turned red from embarrassment. The bell rang loudly signaling the end of the school day. Everyone got up to leave.

"Lauren, can I talk to you for a minute?" Miss Sullivan asked.

"Sure," I said as I finished putting away my books. Most of the students had already left.

"Is everything OK?" Miss Sullivan seemed kind, but there was something sad about her.

"My grandmother broke her arm, and my mom had to go take care of her. I have to stay with Aunt Rose."

"Rowdy Rose?" Miss Sullivan said in horror. "I'm sorry I shouldn't have called her that."

"You know her?"

"We went to high school together. I'm so sorry for you. Let me know if there is anything I can do to help."

"Thanks," I said, grateful for her offer.

"I'll see you tomorrow," Miss Sullivan replied.

"Bye," I said as I walked out of the classroom. I was about to walk home when I remembered that Aunt Rose had said the she wouldn't be home until five because she had an open house or a showing or something. I decided to walk over to the public library and do my homework there until Aunt Rose was home. I didn't want to be alone in the house by myself.

Chapter 6

The library was a two story brick building a few blocks from the school. Miss Gladys Peters greeted me the moment that I walked in through the doors. She was in her early thirties and had short wavy blond hair. She was wearing a navy blue skirt and a buttoned up sweater covered in cat hair. Miss Peters loved cats.

"Lauren, it's so good to see you. Did your mom arrive in California safely?"

"I think so. She's supposed to call me tonight. I miss her a lot."

"I miss her too. How do like staying with your Aunt Rose?"

"It's terrible. I wish I could stay with you."

"I know. I told your mom that you could stay with me, but she was afraid that I lived too far away from your school. The cats and I would have loved your company."

"How are all your cats?"

"They're doing well. I just adopted another one," she said excitedly. "He's orange colored so I named him Cheese Fondue."

"How many cats do you have now?"

"Only five, well six if you count Peanut Butter, but she's such a tiny Siamese, I don't think that she really counts. You'll have to come over and meet my new baby."

"I'd like that." Someone came over to the desk to check out a book, and Miss Peters went to help them. I went up the stairs to the second floor and found a table to do my homework. I was busy working on a math problem when I looked up and saw an old Native American man sitting across from me. He had a long white braid and brown leathery skin. I had talked to him before. He seemed to know a lot about ghosts.

"You seem troubled. Have you seen another spirit?"

"Yes. It was horrifying. There was a little girl hiding under my bed last night. She was holding a knife. I think she wants to hurt me. Can a ghost hurt you?" I asked, distressed.

"Some spirits can be very angry or vengeful over what happened to them while they were alive. They can often generate powerful physical force from those emotions."

"So she can hurt me."

He paused for a moment. "Yes," he finally replied, but I already knew the answer to that question as I reached down to feel the cut on the back of my leg.

"How can I make her go away?"

"She must find peace in order to move on."

"How do I help her find peace?"

"You must find out what she wants."

"She asked me where her mommy was. Do you think that's what she wants?"

"Perhaps. Everything will be made clear to you in time."

"Is that before or after she hurts me again?" I said, frustrated. It wasn't like you could have a conversation with an evil ghost child when she was chasing you with a knife. I didn't get another chance to ask him a question before he got up and silently walked away.

I looked at my watch. It was 4:30 pm. I'd better hurry back to the house before my aunt got home and found out that I wasn't there. It took me about twenty minutes to walk from the library back to the house, and my aunt's car was already in the driveway. I dreaded going inside.

Chapter 7

"Where have you been?" my aunt yelled at me when I walked in the door.

"I went to the library to do my homework."

"You should have told me."

"I'm sorry," I replied.

"Dinner is on the table," Aunt Rose said, and I followed her into the dining room. Poopsie was sitting on her bed nearby. At least she didn't growl at me when I walked into the room. That was an improvement. There was only one plate on the table.

"Aren't you going to eat with me?" I asked.

"I have a date tonight," she replied.

"You're going to leave me alone by myself?" I said, panicked.

"Your mother leaves you alone all the time."

"She never leaves me alone at night," I said, terrified.

"Well, you're a big girl, and you'll be fine. I left my cell phone number by the phone, and you can always call 911 if there's an emergency. Now sit down and eat your dinner before it gets cold." Aunt Rose sat down and placed a bottle of bright red nail polish on the table. She proceeded to touch up her manicure. I reluctantly sat down across from her. I was curious to see what she had made me for dinner. There were small pieces of chicken floating in a pool of grease. Next to it was mashed potatoes with gravy. I bowed my head and silently prayed, "Thank you Lord for this food, may it taste better than it looks." I picked up a piece of chicken with my fork and took a bite. Aunt Rose must have seen the look on my face.

"Is something wrong?" she asked.

"The chicken, it's so...greasy," I finally blurted out.

"The grease helps everything slide right through you," Aunt Rose proclaimed. Poopsie had made her way under the table. Every time Aunt Rose looked down to work on her manicure, I slipped the dog a piece of chicken. Poopsie seemed to like the greasy chicken and lapped it right up. We were slowly becoming friends. I finally took a bite of the mashed potatoes. You could never go wrong with mashed potatoes and gravy. My taste buds were immediately assaulted by the atrocious taste, and it took every ounce of willpower not to spit it out in front of Aunt Rose. Instead of gravy, she had melted peanut butter on top of the potatoes. This was a crime against mashed potatoes. My mother used to say that a way to a man's heart was through his stomach. If that was the case, Aunt Rose was never getting married.

"I'm full," I said as I pushed the offensive food away.

"Good. You can help me pick out an outfit for my date." It sounded like fun, and I was excited as I walked upstairs with Aunt Rose to her bedroom.

"Who are you going out with tonight?" I asked.

"It's someone that I met on the new dating site. His name is Ken, and he's a salesman. He's thirty-five and used to be the quarterback on his high school football team." Aunt Rose disappeared into her closet and pulled out an emerald green dress. "What do you think about this one?"

"That's nice," I replied. She went back into her closet and came back with a dark floral print dress.

"What do you think of this one?"

"That's nice too," I said.

"You're not very helpful," she said, frustrated.

"I'm sorry. I've never been on a date before. I don't know what you're supposed to wear."

"I keep forgetting that you're only nine," Aunt Rose replied.

"Twelve," I corrected her, but she had already disappeared back into her closet. She came back out wearing a red dress.

"That looks really pretty," I said.

"Help me zip it up," Aunt Rose said as she stood in front of me. It was a bit tight on her back side, and I struggled for a while before I could finally get it zipped up. The doorbell rang from downstairs. "Oh, he's here. You should come downstairs with me and meet him." Aunt Rose seemed nervous as she slipped on her strappy sandals and hurried downstairs to open the front door.

"Hello, Rose. It's so nice to meet you. You're even more beautiful than your picture," Ken said as he walked through the front door. He looked far different than I had imagined he would be. He looked like he was closer to fifty-five instead of thirty-five. If he had been a football player, it must have been a long time ago. His stomach hung over his pants, and he smiled at Aunt Rose with what appeared to be fake teeth.

"Ken, this is my niece, Lauren." I wasn't really her niece, but I didn't correct her. Ken barely glanced at me.

"We better get going. I have a reservation at a steakhouse."

"That sounds wonderful. Let me just go upstairs and get my coat." Aunt Rose's high heeled sandals made a loud noise as she walked through the entry way up the stairs. I glanced up at Ken. I didn't like the way he leered at my aunt.

"You're aunt has a nice rear end," he commented. I looked up at Aunt Rose as she climbed the last few stairs. If having a big rear end was nice, then I guess Aunt Rose had a nice one. Either way, it wasn't very nice of him to say so. Mom would say that he was no gentleman. Aunt Rose came down a minute later, and she patted me on the head.

"Be good, Little Quack Quack," she said before she followed Ken outside and closed the front door. I stood in the foyer for a minute. The silence was deafening. Despite all the lights being on, there was a dark, ominous presence that seemed to pervade the house. A shrill sound startled me, and I jumped. It took me a moment to realize that it was the telephone ringing. I went into the kitchen and picked up the phone.

"Hello?"

"Hi, Pumpkin. It's Mom. How are you?" She sounded tired.

"Oh Mom, it's been terrible. The food is disgusting, and the house is haunted." I could hear Grandma yelling in the background. It was something about Mom hiding all her liquor.

"I'm sorry. I can barely hear you. How was your first day of school?"

"It was fine. Miss Sullivan is my new teacher, and she seems really nice."

"Did you get all your homework done?"

"Yes, I already did it." I heard a loud crashing sound on the other end of the phone line. "What's that noise?"

"Grandma is very angry, and she's throwing things. I'm sorry, Pumpkin. I have to go now. I love and miss you so much."

"But Mom, I haven't told you about the evil little girl that's trying to hurt me." I waited for her to answer, but all I heard was the dial tone. She had already hung up. "I really miss you too, Mom," I said into the phone before I hung up. A minute later the phone rang again.

"Mom?" I was sure that she had called me back so that we could talk longer. I waited for her to answer, but all I heard was static on the other end. "Mom?" I asked again. I could barely hear someone talking. "What did you say? I can't hear you," I said loudly.

This time the voice was much clearer. "Why are you in my house?" the little girl's voice whispered to me over the phone. It was followed by a malevolent laugh that filled me with terror. I quickly hung up the phone and hid under the kitchen table, expecting to see the little girl come into the room with a knife at any moment. I wasn't sure how long I sat there, trembling with fear under the table, before Poopsie came over to find out what was wrong with me. I stroked her head for a few minutes before I finally decided what to do next. It was getting late, and I was tired. I decided to run upstairs and sleep in Aunt Rose's room. It seemed to be a safe place. I hoped that once Aunt Rose found me asleep in her bed, she would let me spend the rest of the night there.

I slowly made my way out from under the table and peered into the entry way. No one was there. The whole house was silent. Poopsie followed me toward the stairs. She suddenly started barking and growling at something at the top of the stairs. I looked up, and I thought I saw a flash of white, but I wasn't sure.

"Poopsie, can you see ghosts too?" I asked. She just tilted her head and gave me a confused look. "Do you want to come upstairs with me? Come on girl," I encouraged her. Poopsie turned around and ran as fast as she could away from me. I guess I was on my own. I looked up one last time to make sure that no one was up there. Then I hurried up the stairs and turned down the hallway to my aunt's bedroom. Thankfully, the light was still on. There were scattered dresses laid across the bed, and I put them on a chair. I found my pajamas from this morning in the upstairs bathroom. I quickly put them on and then brushed my teeth. I turned the bedside lamp on and climbed into bed. I waited to hear any sounds, but the house remained eerily silent.

I didn't know what time it was when I heard a loud sound downstairs. I must have fallen asleep, and I rubbed my bleary eyes. The room was cold, and I could see the hairs standing up on my arms. The noises continued. It sounded like someone was walking around down there.

"Aunt Rose, is that you?" I called out loudly. No one answered. "Aunt Rose?" I was sure someone was down there. What if someone had broken into the house? I finally got up the courage to go and check. As I stepped out of bed, the icy chill of the room hit me full force, and I shivered in my thin cotton pajamas. I peered out of the bedroom doorway into the hall. It appeared empty, but it was so dark that it was difficult to tell if someone was hiding in the shadows. I tiptoed over to the banister and carefully looked down to see if anyone was there. I could hear footsteps coming into the foyer. Someone was down there, and I was terrified. Suddenly, a tall woman in a long gray dress walked through the entryway and sat down in front of the organ. She began playing a haunting piece on the organ. Her fingers moved across the keys in a demented manner, playing the same unearthly melody over and over again. I didn't think that she had seen me, and I decided to back away before she did. I took a step back, and the floor board beneath my foot creaked loudly. The sound echoed through the house. The lady in gray abruptly stopped playing and turned around. She looked up, and her crazed eyes looked directly into mine. "I told you to run away and never come back. Now it's too late." She turned back around and dramatically raised her hands above the organ. Then she violently pushed down on all the keys at once, making a deafening sound. I stumbled back and saw a flash of white at the end of the hallway. As I turned to look, I could see the little girl standing there clutching her doll.

"Where's my mommy?" she said as an evil smile spread across her face. Then she raised her hand, and I could see that she was holding a knife. I stood there for a moment in horror before I realized that she was starting to run toward me. I turned and ran blindly down the long hallway toward my aunt's bedroom. I could hear the sound of footsteps behind me. They were getting closer, but I was too afraid to look back. I saw the light coming from my aunt's room, and I quickly raced in and hurried to close the door. As the door was halfway closed, I could see the little girl's gruesome white face in front of me as she hurtled her body against the door. The door pushed back against me and started to open. I let out a bloodcurdling scream as I pushed with all my might to close the door. A moment later it slammed shut, and I fumbled to lock the door with my trembling fingers. The pounding continued on the other side. I took the chair and put it under the door handle and then jumped into bed. The knocking on the door continued. It was interrupted occasionally with her screaming, "Where's my mommy?". My whole body was shaking as I threw the covers over my head and put my hands over my ears to muffle the frightening sounds. I had no idea how long I laid there, scared to death. There were a few minutes of silence followed by the sound of the door handle rattling. She was still trying to get in. There was another knock on the door.

"Lauren, are you in there? Open the door." It was Aunt Rose. Never had I been so happy to hear her voice. I got out of bed and moved the chair away from the door and unlocked it. Aunt Rose walked into the room. She looked angry. "Why did you lock yourself in my bedroom?"

"I heard someone walking downstairs. I thought someone had broken into the house, so I hid in your room."

"No one is here. All the windows and doors were locked when I got home. You should go back to your bedroom."

"Can I sleep with you just one more night?" I begged.

"You're a big girl. You can sleep by yourself."

"Please Aunt Rose, just this one night and I won't ask again," I pleaded. I couldn't go back to the knife wielding little girl's bedroom. "Please, please, please, please, please."

"Just this one night and that's it," she finally agreed.

"Thank you, Aunt Rose." I jumped into her bed before she could change her mind. Aunt Rose went into her closet to change her clothes. "How was your date?" I asked.

She came out of her closet, and she looked enraged. "Do you know that dirty old man tried to grab my bottom at the end of the date?"

"What did you do?" I asked, relieved that her anger was directed at someone else.

"I punched him so hard in the face that his false teeth flew out, and when he went to pick them up, I kicked him in the rear end." A giggle escaped from my mouth before I could stop it. Mom had always taught me that violence was never the answer to anything, but a part of me thought that Ken had deserved it.

"So you're not going to go out on another date?" I asked, hopeful that Aunt Rose would stay home every night from now on.

"Don't worry, Little Quack Quack. I've already met someone else on the dating site, and we plan on going out this weekend." I was disappointed. At least she would be home for a few nights. Aunt Rose turned off the lights and got into bed next to me. When she rolled over, she took most of the covers with her. I pulled what was left of the covers around myself and finally drifted off to sleep.

Chapter 8

"Lauren, get up. You're going to be late for school," Aunt Rose yelled at me. I sat up in bed and looked at the clock. I had overslept. I threw on some clothes and ran downstairs. I took a few bites of cereal and then grabbed a cup of yogurt for lunch.

"Goodbye, Aunt Rose," I said as I went out the front door. I ran all the way to school and made it to my classroom a few minutes before the bell rang. As I got to my desk, I could see that someone had put fake spiders on top of it. I looked around to see who had done it, but most of the kids in the classroom were staring at me, waiting to see my reaction. I was afraid of many things, but my Aunt's haunted house and various ghostly occupants were far scarier than some fake spiders. I scooped up all the plastic spiders on my desk and then dumped them into the waste basket at the front of the classroom. I decided to ignore the whole situation and not let it get to me. My mom had always taught me to pray for and forgive people. I prayed that whoever had done it would get bitten on their bottom by a spider, and then I would feel more forgiving towards them. I decided that was not a very nice prayer and instead just asked the Lord to send my mom home safely as soon as possible.

Miss Sullivan walked into the room just as the bell rang. She looked upset, as if something was weighing very heavily on her mind. She immediately started giving a history lesson on the American Revolution. I enjoyed history and wondered if there were any books on the history of the house that Aunt Rose lived in. I would have to do some research. Miss Sullivan gave a math lesson next before the bell finally rang to go for lunch.

I hadn't seen John this morning to give him the secret signal to meet for lunch. It didn't matter. We were meeting after school to go to Mrs. Harrison's house, and I could tell him about everything that had happened last night on the way over to her house. I ate the cup of yogurt at my locker and went to the school library to see if I could find out about the history of the house. I asked the school librarian for any books that might have any information about houses built in the 1880's in Bozeman. She directed me to a few books in the history section.

I read about John Bozeman who had opened the Bozeman Trail in 1863, which eventually led to the future location of Bozeman. I then skimmed through several of the other books before I finally came across a picture of the house on Raventree Lane. It was a grainy black and white picture with a woman and a man standing in front of it. It was too difficult to tell if the woman was the same lady in gray that I saw playing the organ in the middle of the night. There was only a small paragraph about the house. It was built in 1880 by Thomas Richards who had made his fortune in the oil industry. The house was an example of Queen Anne style architecture. I didn't know what that meant. I guess that's the word they used to describe a creepy mansion. There was no other information about it. The bell rang, and I put the books away and went back to my classroom.

Miss Sullivan gave several more lessons in English, vocabulary, and science. I could hear my stomach rumbling, and I couldn't wait for school to end so that I could get some fresh baked cookies at Mrs. Harrison's house. The school bell finally rang, and I quickly put my school books in my back pack and rushed to the front of school to meet up with John.

"Let's go," John said the second he found me. He looked around to make sure that no one was watching. It wouldn't be good for his reputation if everyone knew that his best friend was a girl. We walked half a block before I finally asked him how his day at school was.

"I got into the advanced math class," John said proudly.

"That's great, John. You've always been good at math."

"How was your day?" John asked.

"Did you know that someone left fake spiders on my desk this morning?"

"Why would somebody do that?" John asked.

"I think I fell asleep in class yesterday and dreamt that the little girl was knocking on the school window with a knife. I jumped up, and when the teacher asked me what was wrong, I told her that I saw a spider."

"Who do you think put the spiders there?"

"I think it might have been Tommy who sits behind me, but I'm not sure," I replied.

"Do you want me to talk to him?" John offered.

"No. It was just a stupid joke, and I threw the spiders away. Besides, I'm not sure that he did it." It meant a lot to me that John wanted to help me.

"OK. Did you see the little girl again last night?"

"Oh, John, it was really horrible. Aunt Rose went out on a date last night and left me all alone. I decided to sleep in her bedroom, and when I woke up, I thought I heard someone walking around downstairs. I went over to the banister and looked to see if someone was down there. A woman wearing a long gray dress walked across the foyer and sat down at the organ. She started playing the spookiest music that I've ever heard."

"What did you do?"

"I tried to walk back quietly to the bedroom before she saw me, but one of the floor boards creaked, and she stopped playing the organ and looked up at me. She said that I should have run when I had the chance and now it was too late. Then the little girl stepped into the dark hallway and asked me, 'Where's my mommy?' and then started chasing me down the hallway with a knife."

"Oh my gosh! Did she hurt you?"

"No, I locked myself in my aunt's bedroom before she could. Aunt Rose finally made it home and said that no one was there. It was really scary. At least I got to sleep in my aunt's bed, and I didn't see the little girl again that night. Who do you think the lady in gray was?" I asked John.

"Do you think she's the little girl's mother?" John replied.

"Why would the little girl ask where her mommy was if her mother was downstairs playing the organ?"

"That's true. Maybe Mrs. Harrison will know." We had just reached her house. It was a two-story Victorian that had been painted pink with blue trim. She was a lonely old widow who baked cookies every afternoon and loved to have company.

"Don't forget, John, to save some cookies for me. There's no food at Aunt Rose's house, and I'm starving to death."

"I will," John replied as he knocked on the front door. An older woman wearing bright purple pants and a leopard print shirt answered the door.

She had recently died her hair pink, and it was almost the exact shade as the color of her house.

"I love your hair, Mrs. Harrison. Pink is my favorite color," I said.

"It's my favorite color too," Mrs. Harrison said happily. "Come in, John and Lauren. It's so good to see you. Be careful not to let the dog out." Mrs. Harrison's dog had died years ago, but everyone humored her.

"We won't," I promised.

"I made sugar cookies with lemon-cream cheese frosting. Would you like some?"

"Yes," John and I said in unison.

"Have a seat. I'll be right back."

"Do you want me to help you?" John asked.

"That's so nice of you to offer, but I was so sure that someone would visit me today that I already set out the plates and a pitcher of sweet tea. Please, help yourself," she said as she disappeared around the corner to the kitchen. John and I sat down, and John poured a glass of tea for me.

"Thanks, John," I said as I settled into an ornate overstuffed chair. This was wonderful. Mrs. Harrison returned a minute later with a plate of warm cookies. The sugar cookie mixed with the lemon-cream cheese frosting was heavenly. I was on my third cookie and John was reaching for his fourth when he leaned forward and passed gas so loudly that it echoed through the living room.

"I'm sorry, what did you just say, John?" Mrs. Harrison asked. I picked up a napkin to hide my laugh. John gave me a dirty look.

"I didn't say anything," he answered.

"My hearing is not that good, but I'm pretty sure that I heard you say something." John's face was turning red from embarrassment.

"He was saying how delicious your cookies are," I said. John looked relieved.

"Thank you, John. I'm so glad that you like them." Mrs. Harrison looked pleased. John nudged me with his foot. I was enjoying the cookies so much that I had almost forgotten why I was there.

"I'm staying with my Aunt Rose while my mom is taking care of my grandmother."

"I'm so sorry to hear that," Mrs. Harrison said sympathetically.

"Aunt Rose recently bought the mansion on Raventree Lane. Do you know anything about the people that used to live there?" I asked.

"Well, I don't want to scare you," Mrs. Harrison paused. "But the house is haunted," she whispered.

"Who's haunting it?" John asked.

"It was originally built by an oil tycoon named Thomas Richards for his wife, Sara, and their child. He went with his child to visit some family and to conduct some business. There was a terrible stage coach accident, and both of them were killed. Every time someone came to the house to tell Sara about their tragic deaths, she would refuse to answer the door and would just play the organ until they left. She continued to play the organ day and night until she went insane. You know, you can't always fix crazy. It's rumored that she still continues to play her haunting music late at night." John's eyes were as wide as saucers. "I'm sorry if I scared you. Have I told an inappropriate story again?"

"No, not at all," I said. The lady in gray was far scarier in person. "Was their child a little girl?" I asked. Maybe John was right and the little girl belonged to the lady in gray.

"No. I'm almost positive it was a boy."

"Do you know if a little blond girl ever lived there?"

"There was little girl that lived there about six or seven years ago."

"Do you remember her name?" I asked.

"Let me think. Her parents were an older couple. They moved into that house when she was just a baby. They mostly kept to themselves. I think their last name was Morgan. Yes, their names were Harold and Sylvia Morgan."

"Do you remember the little girl's name?" John asked.

"She was such a pretty little thing with blond hair and blue eyes. I believe her name was Arabella. Did you know that the word *bella* means beautiful in Italian?"

"I didn't know that," John replied.

"Do you know what happened to her?" I asked.

"Like I said, the Morgans kept to themselves, but I remember hearing a petition read at church that asked everyone to pray for Arabella. She was sick and had been transferred to a special hospital in Billings. She must have been about seven or eight at the time. I don't know what happened to her. Harold Morgan had died a few years before that, and

Sylvia moved out of the house on Raventree Lane not too long after Arabella was hospitalized."

"Do you have any idea where she might have moved to?"

"I'm afraid not, but Sylvia was quite active in the church. Pastor Joe might remember where she moved to. Is there a reason why you want to find them?" Mrs. Harrison asked.

"I was doing some research on the house and the people who used to live there."

"The historical museum in town might have a lot more information on Thomas and Sara Richards who were the original owners. Most of the other families barely stayed a year, you know, with the haunting organ music being played in the middle of the night," Mrs. Harrison winked at me knowingly. I totally understood.

"I'll have to go and check that out. Thanks for all your help, and thank you for the delicious cookies," I replied.

"Yes, thanks for the cookies," John added, and then he walked out the front door.

"Lauren, wait. Let me get you a plate of cookies to take with you. I've heard that Rose is a bit, well...challenged in the kitchen." That was an understatement, I thought. Mrs. Harrison hurried into the kitchen and came back with a small plastic container filled with cookies.

"Thanks again, Mrs. Harrison," I said as she handed me the cookies. Suddenly, she grabbed my hand, and her eyes glazed over. She looked like she was in a deep trance. I tried to pull my hand away, but she had a firm grip on it. She was starting to scare me. The room grew cold, and I started to shiver.

"Are you OK?" I asked worriedly. I tried again to pull away, but she was too strong. I looked up at her, and her pale blue eyes began to turn a dark brown. Her face began to contort into someone that I no longer recognized. "Mrs. Harrison?" I asked, worried that whoever was standing in front of me was no longer Mrs. Harrison. I jumped as she whispered something to me in a deep masculine voice.

"Run, Lauren. Run as fast as you can away from that house and never go back. There's danger there for you." The cuckoo clock chirped loudly, breaking the spell, and Mrs. Harrison released my hand. She smiled as if nothing had happened and said, "Thank you for coming by. I hope that you'll come and visit again soon."

I was too shaken up to answer as I walked away.

"That was weird," I told John once I joined him on the sidewalk.

"It was good news. We found out the little girl's name, and we can ask Pastor Joe at church on Sunday where Sylvia Morgan moved to. Then we just have to get her to come to the house so that Arabella can see her again and move on," John said confidently.

"You think that's all we have to do?" I said, unsure.

"The little girl keeps asking where her mommy is, and we're going to bring her mom to her."

"OK," I agreed. It sounded logical. John always made me feel better, and I was becoming more hopeful that it would work.

Chapter 9

"Wow, that's a big house," John commented as we walked up to the front door of Aunt Rose's house. The door opened suddenly, and Aunt Rose appeared with a scowl on her face.

"Where have you been?" Aunt Rose demanded.

"I invited John over, and we stopped by Mrs. Harrison's house for cookies on the way over," I replied apologetically as I held up the container of cookies. "Would you like some?" I offered, hoping to appease her.

"You should have told me where you were going ahead of time," she said as she yanked the cookies out of my hand.

"I'm sorry," I replied.

"Come inside both of you."

"My mom will be here soon," John replied as he hesitantly stepped into the foyer and looked around.

"Don't worry," I whispered to him. "None of the ghosts are here during the day. They only show up at night." John looked visibly relieved. There was a sudden knock on the door, and it startled both of us. Aunt Rose went to answer it.

"Hi, I'm here to pick up John," a young woman with light brown hair and blue eyes replied.

"Hi, Mom. I'm ready to go," John said as he practically ran out the door.

"Hi, I'm Rose," Aunt Rose replied as she introduced herself to John's mom.

"I'm Emma Taylor, John's mom. It's nice to meet you. Thanks for having John over."

"I was wondering if I could ask you for a favor," Aunt Rose said as she cornered John's mom.

"Sure," Mrs. Taylor answered.

"I have two open houses on Saturday, and I was wondering if you could take Lauren for the day. I'll be home by six o'clock. I'd really appreciate the help."

"Of course, I would love to have Lauren over for the day. We're just planning on catching up on farm chores, but she's welcome to join us."

"I can muck out stalls, help with your chickens, and I can even help clean your house," I said, desperate to spend any time away from the haunted mansion.

Mrs. Taylor laughed. "I'm sure that I can find some fun things for you and John to do also. I'll pick Lauren up around eight in the morning if that's all right."

"That would be perfect for me," Aunt Rose replied.

"Thanks, Mrs. Taylor. I'll see you on Saturday. Thanks for all your help with my project, John. I'll see you at school tomorrow."

"You're welcome," John said as he smiled. "I'll see you tomorrow."

Aunt Rose shut the front door, and I felt a sense of sadness as they left. The sun was starting to set, and I knew that evil was waiting for me in the shadows.

"So is John your boyfriend?" Aunt Rose asked.

"Ewwww, no! We grew up together. He's my friend," I said. "Did you have a boyfriend when you were younger?" I asked.

"There was someone that I loved very much, but it wasn't meant to be," Aunt Rose said sadly. "It's getting late. I'm going to go make dinner."

"Can we order pizza?" I asked as I followed her into the kitchen.

"No, I'm on a diet," Aunt Rose replied as she ate another of Mrs. Harrison's cookies. I was glad that I had stuffed a few of the cookies in my pockets to save for later. Aunt Rose pulled out some frozen dinners and heated them up. We sat at the table, and I said a silent prayer before eating. It wasn't a very large portion of food, but it tasted better than I expected. The phone rang, and I rushed to pick it up, hopeful that it was my mom.

"Hello?"

"Hi, Pumpkin. It's Mom. How are you?"

"I'm fine. How are you?" I asked. I wanted to say so much more, but Aunt Rose was listening.

"It's been a challenge, but Grandma is getting better. How is school?"

"Good. I don't have a lot of homework today. When are you coming home?"

"Soon, I hope. I love you so much, and I miss you every day." Mom sounded on the verge of tears.

"I love you too."

"Here, let me talk to your mom," Aunt Rose said as she grabbed the phone out of my hands. I heard her talking about my nightmares and telling my mom that I was too old to be sleeping with her and that she wouldn't allow it anymore. I knew I had to sleep in the little girl's room tonight, and the thought terrified me.

"I'm going to bed and you should too," Aunt Rose said once she got off the phone.

"OK," I agreed. I had a plan. I went upstairs and put my pajamas on and brushed my teeth and waited for Aunt Rose to go to bed.

"Goodnight, Little Quack Quack," she said as she poked her head into my bedroom.

"Goodnight, Aunt Rose," I replied. Once I heard her bedroom door close, I pulled the blanket and pillow off my bed. I quietly crept downstairs to the parlor and put the blanket and pillow on the couch. I was pretty sure that there were no ghosts in this room, and I'd get up early in the morning before Aunt Rose found out that I was down there. It was dark downstairs, and a part of me worried that I had made a mistake as I curled up onto the couch. I listened for a long time for any spooky sounds, but the house remained silent, and I finally drifted to sleep.

A loud noise woke me in the middle of the night. It was followed by groaning. I was worried that Aunt Rose was hurt. It was dark in the parlor, and I was disoriented as I pulled my blanket off. The frigid cold of the room pierced my skin, and I hesitated to move forward.

"Aunt Rose, are you OK?" I called out. The sound of groaning was even louder this time. I could hear the sound of Poopsie's nails clicking on the wood floor as she walked towards me from the kitchen to find out what was wrong. I knew I had to find out if someone was hurt out there. I wrapped my arms around myself to shield myself from the cold. I crept silently toward the doorway that led into the foyer. I could hear Poopsie following closely behind me. I peered through the doorway, and I tried to adjust my eyes to the dark, but the pillars in the foyer cast long shadows across the room making it difficult to see anything. I could hear groaning coming from the bottom of the stairs, and when I looked, I saw a crumpled body lying at the foot of the stairs.

"Aunt Rose?" I called out in a panic as I ran toward the person lying there. I crouched down, and I could see that it was the old man from my dream. His hand reached out for me. I could feel his bony fingers wrap around my wrist. Sightless brown eyes stared up at me. I recoiled in horror as I tried to pull away, but his grip was too strong for me to pull away.

"Please, let me go. I'll go get some help for you," I begged even though I knew it was too late for him. I could feel shards of ice travel from his bony fingers up my arm, and I started to panic. He pulled me closer, and I could feel his breath on my face. I tried to scream for help, but nothing came out. That's when I finally heard him speak.

"It's too late for me, but not for you. Run," he whispered. "Run as fast as you can and never come back. There's danger here for you." His grip finally loosened as he took his last breath. I heard a sound at the top of the stairs. I looked up and saw the little girl clutching her doll. An evil smile spread across her face. She raised her hand and pointed at me.

"You're next," she said. A wicked laugh escaped from her mouth and echoed through the foyer. I stumbled backwards in horror. I quickly scrambled to get up on shaky legs and ran back to the parlor. I didn't bother to look back as I dove onto the couch and hid under the covers. I could hear someone following closely behind me. A moment later my covers were slightly pulled back, and as I tried to scream, something hard landed on my stomach knocking the wind out of me. I wondered if this is what it felt like to be murdered, and I decided to fight back. I grabbed the heavy weight on my stomach and instantly realized that it was Poopsie. She had jumped under the covers with me and was shaking violently. I tried to soothe her, but I could barely control my own trembling. Poopsie's fetid breath made it nearly impossible to breathe under the covers. I broke out in a cold sweat as I tried to listen for any footsteps, but I couldn't hear anything over the pounding of my heart. I tried to sink further into the couch, knowing that it was no protection from the evil that was coming for me.

That's when I heard the footsteps in the foyer. They were coming closer. It was too late.

There was no way out. I was trapped. I could hear someone at the doorway. I clutched my covers tightly, desperately hoping that they could somehow protect me. Suddenly, I heard a scraping sound nearby as if a chair were being moved. There was a long period of silence as I held my breath, waiting for what would happen next. Without warning, the sound of haunting music from the organ filled the house. The same unearthly melody was being played over and over again. It was the lady in gray. My body continued to shake as I waited for hours for the evil little girl to enter into the parlor, but she never came. The same mournful music played all night until I finally fell asleep from exhaustion.

Chapter 10

"Lauren, Lauren, wake up," Aunt Rose said as she shook my shoulders. I peeked out from under my covers to make sure that it was really her. "What are you doing down here?" she asked.

"Poopsie was scared last night, and I wanted to keep her company," I replied lamely. Poopsie stuck her head out from under the covers. Neither of us could hide the guilty look on our faces. We had become fast friends due to our mutual fear of the ghosts haunting the house.

"Was my little Poopsie scared last night?" Aunt Rose asked as she scooped the dog up and kissed her. "Don't worry, Mommy's here." I actually felt a little jealous of the dog. I missed my mom. "Hurry up and get ready for school or you'll be late," Aunt Rose said as she went into the kitchen to make breakfast with Poopsie tucked safely under her arm.

I peered into the foyer and looked at the bottom of the stairs expecting to see an old man lying there, but no one was there. I ran up the stairs and into my bedroom. I put on a clean pair of jeans and a pink sweater and then hurried down to eat breakfast. A bowl of the same birdseed cereal was put in front of me. My stomach grumbled in protest.

"Did you hear the music last night?" I asked.

"What music?" Aunt Rose said, confused.

"The organ music," I replied.

"There wasn't any organ music. I'm not even sure that organ can be played anymore since it's so old." I decided to drop the subject. She would never believe me anyways.

"I'll see you after school," I said as I picked up my backpack full of books.

"You are coming straight home, aren't you?" Aunt Rose asked.

"Yes," I replied. John and I wouldn't be able to talk to Pastor Joe until Sunday and ask him where Arabella's mom was living. I reassured myself that it was just a few days more until we solved the mystery.

I stepped outside the front door and looked at the sky. It was a gloomy day with dense clouds that hid even the smallest ray of sunshine. I heard an eerie cry, and as I looked up, I could see a raven perching in the tree nearby. A flash of white caught my eye, and I could see the curtain being pulled back from the attic window. A moment later the raven swooped down toward me, and I screamed as I ran as fast as I could to school. I tried to reassure myself that I hadn't seen anything and that the raven was just after the birdseed cereal that I had just eaten, but deep down inside I knew that I was just lying to myself. The haunting words telling me to run as fast as I could and never come back kept playing over in my mind. It took every ounce of strength to stop at my school once I got there and not continue to run on forever.

I only had a second to stop at my locker before the bell rang. I made it into my classroom and sat down at my desk just in time. Miss Sullivan started giving a lesson in science, but my mind kept wandering back to the old man and the little girl from last night. The bell rang for lunch, and I was grateful for the break.

I went to my locker and realized that Aunt Rose hadn't made me a lunch since it was Friday. I had told her that the school served hot lunch on Fridays, but I had forgotten to tell her that there was no hot lunch during the first week of school. I saw John in the hallway, and he motioned for me to come over to his locker.

"Hi, John," I waved.

He looked around to make sure that no one was watching us and then shoved a brown paper bag into my hand. "My mom made this for you," he replied and quickly walked away before anyone saw us together. I looked inside the bag, and I could see that his mom had made a delicious lunch for me. I almost jumped for joy. I wanted to ask John if we could meet in our secret place, but he had already left to join his friends for lunch. I would have to tell him about the old man another day. I was so happy about the food that it didn't matter. I walked over to the lunch tables and saw some girls from my class.

"Hi, Ashley. Hi, Jenny. Is it OK if I sit here?" I asked.

"Sure," Ashley said with little enthusiasm. "Were you just talking to John?" she asked.

"No, not really. His mom made me lunch since I'm staying with my aunt," I replied as I reached into the bag and pulled out a peanut butter and jelly sandwich. I took a bite. Never had a sandwich tasted so heavenly.

"I heard that your aunt bought that old, scary mansion in town. Is it really haunted?" Jenny asked.

I thought about what I was going to say as I chewed the last bite of my sandwich. I knew if I told them the truth, they would think I was either a liar or crazy. I had a different plan. "Mrs. Harrison told me that the house was originally built by a rich man for his wife and son. The man and his son died in a carriage accident and when they went to tell his wife, she refused to listen. She would just play the organ day and night until she went crazy. Some people say that you can still hear the organ music playing in the middle of the night."

"That's really scary, Lauren," Ashley said, visibly upset.

"Yeah," Jenny agreed. "I'm never coming over to your house."

"But it's not my house. It's my aunt's house, and I'm only there for a little while," I explained, but it didn't matter. The two girls had gotten up from the table and left. I always seemed to say the wrong thing. I reached into my lunch bag and pulled out a homemade blueberry muffin. At least the food was good.

The school bell finally rang, and I went inside and sat at my desk. Miss Sullivan gave us a spelling test, and I think I did well. It was followed by an English lesson and a lecture on the American Revolution. It was finally time to go home, and I packed up my books.

"Lauren, can I talk to you before you leave?" Miss Sullivan asked me.

"Sure," I said. I wasn't sure what she wanted. Most of the students had already left as I walked over to her desk.

"Some of the girls in your class told me that you were scaring them with ghost stories? Is that true?" she asked.

My face turned bright red. "They asked me if my aunt's house was haunted, and I told them the story that Mrs. Harrison told me about the ghost that plays the organ in the middle of the night."

"Oh, the lady in grey," she said excitedly. "I've heard that story before. When I was in high school someone dared me to go knock on the front door of that haunted house late at night. The house was vacant, but when I ran up to the door, I heard the scariest organ music being played inside. I ran away and never told anyone about it."

"I've heard it too," I admitted hesitantly.

"You have? Well, let's keep that between ourselves," she said as she smiled at me. "Some people just don't understand."

"OK. Thanks, Miss Sullivan," I said as I leaned forward and hugged her. She hugged me back, and it reminded me of how much I missed my mom. Miss Sullivan would make a great mom. "Do you have any kids?" I asked. Miss Sullivan was silent for a moment. A sorrowful expression briefly flashed across her face before she answered.

"I consider all of you my children," she smiled, but the smile never reached her eyes. "You better hurry home. I wouldn't want you to get in trouble with Rose. I'll see you on Monday."

"Bye," I said as I skipped out the door. I walked home slowly. I wasn't looking forward to spending more time in the haunted house. I hesitated outside the front door before I finally went inside.

"Hi, Little Quack Quack," Aunt Rose said as I closed the front door. "I thought maybe I would order a pizza and we could watch a movie."

"We can really have pizza? I thought you were on a diet."

"I've gained five pounds on my diet. I figure if I'm going to gain weight, it might as well be with food that I enjoy," Aunt Rose admitted.

"Yay! Pizza!" I cheered as I jumped up and down. I didn't even care what toppings she ordered. A half hour later the pizza arrived. It was a deep dish pizza with extra cheese and mushrooms. "This is so good. Thanks, Aunt Rose," I said with a mouthful of pizza. I was on my fourth slice when Aunt Rose went over to put in the DVD. "What are we going to watch?" I asked.

"Sense and Sensibilty. It's my favorite movie."

"What is it about?"

"It's based on a Jane Austen novel. It's about a widow and her three daughters who are left destitute when their father dies. It's a love story."

"It doesn't sound like a love story," I replied as I snuggled under a blanket on the couch. I had eaten so much pizza that I could barely keep my eyes open. The movie started, and I thought that the scenery was beautiful and so were the dresses. I saw the part where Elinor was falling in love with Edward, but then she had to move away with her family to live with relatives. That's where Marianne met Willoughby and fell in love. I thought he was very handsome. That was the last thing I remembered before I fell asleep.

I woke late at night to the sound of haunting music. The mournful melody coming from the organ seemed to echo through the house. I looked around and realized that I had fallen asleep on the couch. Aunt Rose must have gone upstairs. Poopsie jumped onto the couch and burrowed under the covers. The music must have scared her. "It's all right, Poopsie. It's just the lady in grey," I reassured her although I was petrified myself. The television was still on, but there was just static on the screen. I tried to find the remote control to turn it off, but it must have fallen under the couch. I got up to turn it off, and as I took a few steps toward the television, I thought I heard someone calling my name.

"Lauren," the voice whispered. "Lauren, come here." Paralyzing fear gripped me, and I stood frozen in place. The voice was getting louder. "Lauren, come here," the voice demanded more loudly. I strained my ears to hear where the voice was coming from. "Lauren, I'm right here." Complete terror consumed me as I realized the voice was coming from the television. An image was beginning to materialize on the screen. I willed myself to move but stood there motionless staring at the screen. The dog barked behind me, breaking the trance that I was in. I lunged forward and turned off the television. The room was dark again. "It's all right now, Poopsie," I said as I turned to go back to the couch.

There was the sound of a small click, and I could hear the static from the TV behind me. The television had been turned back on. I was afraid to turn around again. I stood there for a minute with the light from the television casting a shadow of me on the wall. I looked like a monster. My heart was pounding. I didn't know how long I stood there before I got up enough courage to turn around. As I slowly looked behind me, I could see that it was just static. I took a few hesitant steps toward the television. I quietly leaned forward to try to unplug the television when a picture of the little girl came on. Her eyes glowed as a wicked smile spread across her face. A sinister laugh escaped, and it was filled with such malevolence and evil that I stepped back in horror. Her mouth opened wide, and she began to speak. "Where's my mommy?" she said. I stood there for a moment, frozen in fear. Then she reached her hand out toward me, and I could see the glint of a knife. As she reached farther forward, I could see her hand and arm begin to emerge from the television. She was coming out. A silent scream escaped from me as I hurled myself forward and pulled the cord from the wall. The room was plunged back into darkness. I scrambled to get back up and took a flying leap onto the couch. Poopsie yelped as I accidently knocked her. I pulled the covers over my head and trembled in fear as the disturbing organ music played around me. I covered my ears to muffle the sounds of the demented notes being played. The parlor wasn't safe from ghosts. I wasn't sure that any room in this house was.

Chapter 11

"Lauren, get up. Mrs. Taylor is going to be here soon to pick you up." I crawled out from under the covers on the couch. I hadn't slept much, and I was exhausted.

"What happened in the movie last night? Did Elinor marry Edward?" I asked.

"Yes, she did," Aunt Rose replied.

"I thought so. Did Marianne marry the good-looking guy, Willoughby?" I asked as I took a slice of cold pizza from the refrigerator to eat for breakfast.

"No, they didn't get married."

"Why not? I thought they loved each other."

"Willoughby was disinherited by his aunt. Since he didn't have any money, he decided to marry a wealthy woman who could support him instead."

"But what happened to Marianne?"

"She married Colonel Brandon," Aunt Rose said as she poured her coffee.

"Colonel Brandon, the old guy in the movie? She married the old guy?" I asked, confused.

"Colonel Brandon truly loved her, and she grew to love him. Sometimes second chances at love are even better than the first," Aunt Rose explained. "You better hurry and change. Emma Taylor will be here in a few minutes."

"OK," I said as I headed upstairs. Love was confusing. I ran upstairs and pulled on a pair of jeans and a sweater. I heard the doorbell ring and hurried downstairs to open the door.

"Hi, Lauren," Mrs. Taylor said as John stood next to his mom on the doorstep. "Are you ready to go?" she asked.

"Yes," I said excitedly.

"Hi, Emma. Hi, John," Aunt Rose said as she joined me at the door.

"Hi, Rose. I'll bring Lauren home after we finish dinner," Mrs. Taylor replied.

"That sounds great. I really appreciate your help," Rose said as she patted me on the head. "I'll see you later. Be good, Little Quack Quack." John snickered, and my face turned red. I stepped outside, and Rose closed the front door.

"Why does she call you Little Quack Quack?" John asked as we walked toward the car.

"I have no idea," I lied. John knew most of my secrets, but that was one that he would never find out.

"Is there anything that you need to pick up at your house?" Mrs. Taylor asked me.

"Yes. I'd like to get a few things, if that's OK."

"Of course. We'll stop there first."

The farm had never looked so beautiful to me. It was a clear day. The temperature was starting to cool down, but I could feel the warmth of the sun on my face as I stepped out of the car. Susie hurried over to the fence to greet me. I ran towards her and wrapped my arms around her neck.

"I've missed you so much," I said to her as I tried to hold back tears. I knew John and his mom were waiting for me, so I quickly went into the barn and got Susie a cup of oats. She greedily ate them. I threw some mealworms into the chicken coop. Even the chickens were happy to see me. I didn't want to leave. I reluctantly walked towards the house and found the spare key in the flower pot. I went into the kitchen and put a box of cereal and some snacks into a bag. Then I headed upstairs and picked out a dress and shoes for church. I went back downstairs and locked up the house and got back into the car.

"Thanks, Mrs. Taylor."

"You're welcome, Lauren. Have you eaten breakfast?" she asked.

"I had pizza," I replied.

"Rose fed you pizza for breakfast?" she asked, dismayed.

"Yes. It's the best breakfast I've had since I've been there," I replied happily.

"Mom, we should have pizza for breakfast," John said enthusiastically.

"I don't think so," Mrs. Taylor replied firmly. We had just arrived at John's house. "John, the stalls need to be cleaned out, and the horses need some fresh hay. Lauren, you're welcome to help John or you can join me in the house. I'm making pies today."

"I'll help John," I said. I had a lot to tell him. John smiled. He seemed glad that I wanted to help him.

"All right. Come back to the house when you're finished. I should have lunch ready by then,"

Mrs. Taylor replied as she went up the porch stairs and opened the front door.

"OK," John replied. Moose came bounding out of the house and jumped on me. "Moose, down," John commanded. Moose was too excited to listen, and I loved the attention.

"Hi, Moose. I've missed you too," I replied happily.

"You haven't brought any weird hats or outfits for Moose today, have you?" John asked.

"Not today, but I will next time," I said as I smiled. We started walking toward the barn together. It was a large red barn that had to have been at least a hundred years old.

"Have you seen the little girl again?" John asked.

"Yes. I've seen her twice. It was really scary. Last night I fell asleep on the couch watching a movie, and when I woke up the little girl was trying to talk to me through the TV. I swear I saw her hand and arm start to come out of the television before I ran and unplugged it."

"Wow. That's like out of a horror movie," John replied, terrified.

"I know. I also saw her the night before that. I decided to sleep downstairs in the living room. I thought it would be safer there, but in the middle of the night, I heard a loud noise in the entry way, and it sounded like someone was in a lot pain. I thought it was Aunt Rose, but I found an old man at the bottom of the stairs. He grabbed my arm and told me to run before it was too late, and then I think he died. That's when I saw the little girl at the top of the stairs, and she pointed at me and said, 'You're next,' and then laughed," I said. Chills ran up my spine just talking about it.

"What did you do next?" John asked.

"I ran back to the couch and hid under the covers with Poopsie. I thought that the little girl would find me, but she never did. I just heard the sound of organ music playing for the rest of the night."

"Did you find the old man in the morning?" John asked.

"No. There was no one there. Who do you think he is?" I wondered.

"I guess he could be Arabella's father. Maybe she pushed him down the stairs and killed him," John replied.

"That's horrible," I said, but I had thought the same thing myself.

"After we clean up the barn, we can look on the computer to find out if there is any information on the Morgan family," John suggested.

"That's a great idea," I replied.

"Of course it is," John said as he smiled. We both got to work cleaning out the barn. It was the first time in a long time that I felt at peace. When we finally finished, we headed back to the house.

"Hi, Mom," John said as the screen door slammed behind us. "Is lunch ready?"

"Yes. Why don't you two go wash up and then you can help me set the table." We took turns in the bathroom and then put plates and utensils on the table. Mrs. Taylor put a bowl of homemade potato salad on the table with a platter of fried chicken and biscuits.

"Wow. This looks so delicious," I exclaimed.

"Thank you, Lauren," Mrs. Taylor replied. We bowed our heads and said grace before I loaded my plate with the mouthwatering food. I barely said a word as I savored every bite.

"Mom, is it OK if Lauren and I use the computer to do some homework?" John asked.

"Of course. You can use the computer in your dad's office when you're finished," Mrs. Taylor replied. "Although I think Lauren would like seconds, wouldn't you?"

"Yes, please...and maybe thirds," I replied.

"I'm glad that you're enjoying the food so much," Mrs. Taylor said as she laughed.

"Best food I've had in forever," I said as I took another bite of a buttery biscuit. By the time I finished, I had to loosen my belt. I helped John clear the table and put the dishes in the sink. "Thanks again, Mrs. Taylor, for such an incredible meal."

"You're welcome. You two can go over to the office while I finish putting the dishes in the dishwasher." John and I went into a room with a desk piled with papers and a computer. I pulled up a chair next to him.

"I think we should try and find out where Sylvia Morgan is first," John replied as he typed her name into the computer.

"OK," I replied. Her name popped up on the screen. There was a Sylvia Morgan listed in Bozeman, Montana. She was 58 years old, and there were two addresses listed for her in Bozeman and one in Missoula. "Can you get the exact address that she's at now?" I asked John. John tried to click on the link, but it said that you had to pay with a credit card to find out the addresses.

"I can't get them unless I use a credit card. Pastor Joe might know where she is, and if he doesn't, then I'll ask my mom if I can use her credit card," John replied.

"OK. What about Harold Morgan? What happened to him?" I asked. John entered his name into the computer. He scrolled down and then clicked on one of the articles. "What does it say?"

"This is an obituary written nine years ago about Harold Morgan. It says that Harold Morgan, 59, of Bozeman, Montana passed away at his home on September 15, 2007 from a heart attack. He is survived by his wife Sylvia and daughter Arabella. A graveside service will be held at 11 a.m. on Thursday at the Bozeman Cemetery."

"It didn't say anything about him falling down the stairs?"

"No, nothing," John replied.

"Maybe I was just having a bad dream about the man who fell down the stairs," I said, confused.

"I don't know. Maybe she did push him down the stairs, but her mother tried to cover it up. We can find out more about it once we find Sylvia Morgan," John reassured me.

"What about Arabella? What happened to her?" I asked. John typed in her name, but nothing came up.

"I can't find anything on her," John replied.

"Mrs. Harrison said that she was sent to another hospital out of town. Maybe she died in another city," I commented.

"That's right. I'll try all the major cities in Montana." John typed in other cities, but after an hour of looking, no information came up.

"Her mother could have transferred her to another hospital out of state," I suggested.

"I guess or maybe her mother realized that Arabella had pushed her father down the stairs and murdered him. She was so horrified over having an evil daughter that she accidently killed Arabella and buried her in the backyard. Now Arabella wants you to find her mother so that she can get revenge on her," John replied.

"That's a terrible story, and why does there always have to be a body buried in the backyard? I'm already scared as it is," I said, upset.

John apologized. "I'm sorry. We'll find out tomorrow from Pastor Joe where Sylvia is, and then we can ask her to come over to the house. Once Arabella sees her mom, she can move on," John reassured me.

"All right," I said. I sincerely hoped that John was right, but now I was afraid of the backyard.

"Do you want to go fishing?" John asked as he closed the computer.

"Only if you put the worms on the hook," I said.

"Sure," John said as a smile lit up his face. Fishing was one of John's favorite things to do. I didn't enjoy it as much, but it made John happy. John got two fishing rods from the garage and handed me the tackle box to carry to the river. We walked over to the Gallatin River that bordered the farm and found a good spot to fish. John got the fishing rods ready.

"Let me show you how to cast again," John said. "You need to push this button first and then cast the line." The last time I forgot to push the button, the fishing line didn't go very far and caught John on the back of his shirt. "Now you try," John said as he handed me the rod. He stepped far away from me.

"I think I got it," I said after a few tries. We stood there in silence fishing for a while. I felt a small tug on the end of my line. "I think I have a fish," I said excitedly.

"Slowly reel it in," John instructed. He went and grabbed a net. I slowly reeled the fish in, and John scooped it into the net.

"Did you see that? I caught a fish," I said as I jumped up and down. "I caught a fish."

"Yes, you did, but it's too small to keep. I'm going to throw it back," John said as he carefully took the hook out of the fish and put it back in the water. I watched it swim away. John and I fished for another hour, and John caught two large trout. I got a few nibbles but didn't catch any more fish.

"We should go home now," John said as he started to pack up.

"That was fun. Did you know that's the very first fish that I've ever caught?"

"You did great," John replied as he smiled at me. He was glad that I had enjoyed fishing so much. We walked back to the house, and I could smell apple pie baking in the oven. It smelled heavenly.

"Mom, I caught two trout," John said proudly.

"That's wonderful, John. I'll fry them up for dinner," Mrs. Taylor said as she took the fish. "Why don't you two get cleaned up and help me out." I washed up and then helped cut up some vegetables for a salad. John's dad came in from working in the field. "Dinner is ready. Let's sit down and eat." We said grace, and I filled my plate with food. It was a wonderful dinner filled with laughter and delicious food. I took my time eating dessert, hoping to delay going back to the haunted mansion. I was having such a good time that I didn't want to leave.

"I can't believe it's almost seven. I must have lost track of time. I promised to have you back at your aunt's house by now. I'll call her and tell her that we're on our way," Mrs. Taylor said as she got up from the table.

"Thank you for a wonderful meal," I said as I started to help clear the table.

"Don't worry about that, Lauren. We should get going. John can finish cleaning up," Mrs. Taylor replied. I gathered the bags that I had collected from my house and walked to the car.

"Bye, John," I said sadly. "I'll see you at church tomorrow."

"See you later," John said as he waved back.

Mrs. Taylor and I sat in silence on the car ride over to my aunt's house. The warmth and joy that I had felt with the Taylor family was immediately extinguished the moment that we pulled into the driveway. In the dark of night, the ominous feeling that pervaded the house was overwhelming. The ravens that perched in the tree looked like gargoyles protecting their lair. The curtain in the attic window was pulled back, and I knew that I was being watched. Suddenly, a flood of light filled the entry way, and I could see Aunt Rose step outside to greet us.

"Did you have a good time, Little Quack Quack?" Aunt Rose asked.

"I had a really good time," I replied. "Thanks, Mrs. Taylor."

"You're welcome."

"Thank you for taking Lauren today. The weekends are so hectic for me," Rose commented.

"It was my pleasure. Lauren is a wonderful girl, and I'd be more than happy to take care of her any time," Mrs. Taylor replied as I retrieved my bags out of the car and slammed the door shut.

"Thanks again," Aunt Rose said. Mrs. Taylor started to drive away. "So what did you do today?" she asked as she ushered me inside.

"I helped clean out the barn and then went fishing with John. I caught my very first fish," I said excitedly.

"That's disgusting. No wonder you look so filthy. The first thing you have to do is go straight upstairs and take a shower."

"OK," I said as I picked up my bags. I took a quick glance at the top of the stairs expecting to see the little girl standing there, but the stairway was empty. I breathed a sigh of relief and went upstairs. I dropped the bags off in my bedroom and took a towel out of the hallway closet. The bathroom had a large clawfoot tub with a shower curtain around it. I turned on the hot water and waited for it to warm up before I stepped inside. The warm water felt good, and I spent a long time trying to scrub off all the dirt. Aunt Rose had some special shampoos and conditioners that smelled wonderful. I lathered up my hair and hoped that there was a bottle that could help with the tangles in my hair. The bathroom seemed chilly so I turned up the hot water. Suddenly, the sound of footsteps outside the bathroom door startled me.

"Aunt Rose, is that you?" I called out. No one answered back. The door knob began to rattle. "Aunt Rose?" I asked again. The door creaked open, and a slight breeze gently shifted the shower curtain. "Aunt Rose?" I asked one more time, and then I heard the door click shut again. I began to shiver. Someone was in the bathroom with me. I listened for any footsteps, but I couldn't hear anything over the sound of the water. I stood frozen in fear, unsure of what I should do next. The hot water was running out, and my teeth began to chatter loudly. I had no choice but to get out. I turned off the shower and waited. I half expected someone to rip the shower curtain open and attack me. Instead I just heard silence. I told myself that it was just my imagination, but the feeling of a dark, malevolent presence in the room was too strong to ignore. I cautiously pulled the shower curtain back and peered into the bathroom. The room was shrouded in a hazy fog from the steam. It cast an otherworldly glow. I quickly glanced around, but other than the dirty clothes scattered on the floor, the room was empty. I let out the breath that I had been holding in, but the feeling that there was something evil in the room remained. I wrapped the towel around my body and went to the bathroom sink to brush my teeth. The mirror was fogged, and I wiped it with a small hand towel on the sink. Horror gripped me as two blue eyes that were not my own stared back at me through the mirror. A twisted, wicked smile appeared on her face, and her evil laugh echoed through the bathroom. Before I could run away, the little girl's hand reached out from the mirror and grabbed my wrist. Terror coursed through my body as a muffled scream escaped from my mouth. I pulled my arm back, but her grip was too strong, and she began pulling me towards her. My feet began to slip from under me as

I was propelled forward. The momentum caused me to slam my fist into the mirror. The mirror shattered into pieces. The sound of glass breaking echoed through the house.

"What happened?" Aunt Rose yelled as she came running into the bathroom.

"I'm sorry. I slipped when I got out of the shower and broke the mirror." I couldn't stop trembling, and I braced my hands on either side of the sink to steady myself.

"Is that blood?" Aunt Rose screamed as she pointed to one of my hands.

"I must have cut myself on the mirror," I replied as I watched blood trickle down one of my fingers into the sink.

"Oh my goodness, that's blood. I think I'm going to be sick," Aunt Rose said as the color drained from her face. She quickly sat down on the toilet seat. "What should I do? Should I take you to the hospital?"

"No. It's just a small cut. I'm sure I can just put a band aid on it."

Aunt Rose looked at my hand again. "Oh my goodness, that's a lot of blood. I don't feel well. I think I'm going to faint." Aunt Rose put her head between her legs and started taking deep breaths. I wrapped the hand towel around my finger and put pressure on it to stop the bleeding.

"Why don't you go lie down, Aunt Rose. I'll bandage my finger and clean up all the blood and broken pieces of mirror," I suggested. I was worried that she was going to pass out.

"That's a good idea. As soon as you are done cleaning up here, bring me a cold compress for my head," she said as got up and walked feebly back to her bedroom.

The bleeding had stopped, and I cleaned the cut as best as I could. I found a band aid in the medicine cabinet and wrapped it around my finger. I cautiously picked up the pieces of the mirror and put them in the waste basket, careful not to cut myself on the jagged edges. Once everything was cleaned up, I found another hand towel in the linen closet, and I wet it down with cold water. My trembling had finally stopped, and I brought the towel over to my aunt's room.

"Here you go, Aunt Rose," I said as I draped the wet cloth across her forehead.

"Thank you. That feels good. Now, can you go down stairs and get a shot glass and fill it with whiskey for me? That will help calm my nerves. It's all been too much for me," she replied dramatically.

"Sure. I'll be right back." I didn't know what a shot glass was. Mom never drank, not even a glass of wine. I decided to take one of the tall glasses from the kitchen cabinet. I went over to the liquor cabinet and tried to figure out which bottle had the word whiskey written on it. A large bottle with amber liquid finally caught my eye. This was the right one, and I carefully poured the liquid into the glass until it was almost full. I was quite proud of myself for accomplishing the task. My aunt was not as pleased with me when I finally returned to her bedroom.

"Lauren, that's the wrong glass. That's way too much whiskey," she protested.

"I can pour some back into the bottle," I offered.

"No. I'll just have a few sips," she replied.

"OK," I said as I handed her the glass. I left her bedroom before she could yell at me some more. I put on a clean pair of pajamas and brushed my teeth. I heard the phone ring and ran downstairs. I hadn't talked to my mom today, and I wanted to tell her about my day. I picked up the phone. There was static on the other end. "Mom, is that you?" I asked. I could barely hear a voice coming through. "I can't hear you." The voice on the other end was much louder this time. Sheer terror overwhelmed me the moment that I realized who was on the phone.

"What are you doing in my house?" the little girl's voice demanded. I slammed the phone down immediately. I stared at it for a moment as if it were a snake that was going to strike. The phone rang again, and I jumped. I quickly ran up the stairs to my aunt's room. Aunt Rose was passed out on the bed and snoring. The glass of amber liquid was almost empty. She still had all her clothes on and one of her house slippers.

"Aunt Rose," I said as I took off her slipper. I was going to beg her to let me sleep with her, but she continued to snore. I pinched her big toe, but she barely stirred. I figured I could sleep next to her and she'd never know it. I left all the lights on and crawled under the covers. I fell asleep a few minutes later. I vaguely remembered waking to the sounds of organ music being played in the middle of the night. I recalled Mrs. Harrison saying that you can't always fix crazy, and I wasn't sure that there was anything that I could do to help the lady in grey. I put my hands over my ears to muffle the mournful sounds and went back to sleep.

Chapter 12

I woke up early the next morning. Sunlight poured through the bedroom window. Everything always seemed less scary in the bright light. I slowly crawled out from under the blankets, careful not to wake Aunt Rose, and then tiptoed out of the room. I found the box of cereal that I had brought from my house and went into the kitchen. Poopsie greeted me happily, knowing that I would smuggle her any scraps of leftover food that I had. I gave her a piece of cheese from the refrigerator and pulled out the milk for my cereal. It was a big improvement over the birdseed that I usually had every morning. After finishing my breakfast, I went upstairs to get ready for church. I put on a pink dress and white sandals. I grabbed the pink, plastic purse that Mom had bought me for Easter, and I went into my aunt's room.

"Aunt Rose," I called to her. She was still asleep in the same awkward position that she had been in since last night. "Aunt Rose," I said more loudly. She barely stirred. Her big toe was sticking out, and I pinched it as hard as I could.

"What? What's wrong?" Aunt Rose said as she bolted upright in bed.

"We're going to be late for church," I replied.

"What time is it?" Aunt Rose asked.

"Eight thirty, but you're already dressed. You just have to put your shoes on," I suggested optimistically. Aunt Rose's hair was sticking up, and her eyes were bloodshot. It would take more than shoes to make her look presentable.

"Stop yelling. My head hurts," Aunt Rose said as she glared at me. I wasn't even talking loudly, but I decided not to say anything at all. "Give me a few minutes, and I'll be ready," she finally conceded.

"I'll wait for you downstairs," I whispered and then left the room. Twenty minutes later Aunt Rose came into the kitchen. Her hair was damp from having showered, and she was wearing a floral dress.

"I need some aspirin and coffee before we leave," she growled. I just kept silent, afraid that she would yell at me again. We were going to be late no matter what I said. When we finally arrived, everyone was already seated, and the service was nearly half way over. I felt embarrassed as a few people looked up at us before we found a seat in the back of the church.

Pastor Joe stood at the front of the church. He was a tall, thin man in his sixties with kind, blue eyes. His wife had passed away several years ago, and he liked to keep busy helping people in the parish. He began his sermon. He talked about loving your enemies and praying for those who persecute you. He said that it was easy to love someone who loved you, but if you wanted to be like Jesus, you had to be good to everyone. That was easier said than done, especially if you were dealing with Aunt Rose or an evil ghost child. Pastor Joe said that at the very least you should pray for someone that you didn't like. It would change them as much as it changed you. I decided to pray for Arabella and Aunt Rose.

I didn't hear anything else that Pastor Joe said. Someone in the front row was snoring loudly. I sat up straighter to see who it was, and I could see a little pink head leaning backwards in the pew. Mrs. Harrison might be dainty, but she snored louder than a freight train. A loud laugh was heard coming from the side of the church, and when I looked over, I could see John's mom slap him on the back of his head. I put my hand over my mouth to muffle my own laugh. At least I wasn't the only one who got into trouble today. Thankfully, the rest of the service was short, and as soon as it ended, I headed outside to the table filled with donuts. I put my allowance money into a donation basket and started filling my purse with donuts.

"Are you stealing all the donuts?" a voice asked. It startled me.

"John, you scared me. I put all my allowance money in the basket. Besides, Aunt Rose doesn't have any good food, and I'm starving."

"OK. I'll stand in front of you and tell you when someone is coming," he suggested.

"Thanks, John." He was a good friend. I put a few jelly donuts and an apple fritter in my purse before John stopped me.

"Pastor Joe is coming over," John said frantically. I slammed my purse shut and tried to look innocent.

"Hi, John and Lauren. How are you today?" Pastor Joe asked.

"Fine," we both said in unison.

"I heard that your aunt bought the old mansion on Raventree Lane. How do you like staying there?" he asked.

"It's spooky," I replied. I remembered that I was supposed to ask him about Sylvia Morgan. "Did you know the Morgans? They lived there about ten years ago."

"I'm sorry. I was at another parish ten years ago." I felt devastated by the news.

John immediately rallied for me. "What about Sylvia Morgan? Mrs. Harrison said that Sylvia was involved in the church. Is she still helping out here?" John asked. I was grateful that he was here with me.

"Actually, I do know Sylvia Morgan. I met her a few years ago when I started doing church services at the Oakdale Convalescent Hospital. She's a patient there. Why do you ask?"

"I just wanted to know more about the house, and I thought that she might know since she used to live there," I lied.

"I'm afraid that she might not be very helpful. She has Alzheimer's disease, and her memory seems to come and go. You would be better off doing your research at the library. I'm sorry that I couldn't help you more. It was good seeing you both. Don't eat too many donuts, Lauren," Pastor Joe said as he winked at me and walked away. My face turned bright red.

"I know where that convalescent hospital is. My grandmother used to stay there. It's only a few blocks from the school," John said excitedly.

"Do you think we can go there tomorrow after school?" I asked.

"Sure. I'll ask my mom if it's OK."

"Thanks, John." I was actually feeling hopeful again.

"I have to go," John said as his mother was waving to him to come over.

"I'll see you tomorrow."

"See you," he replied as he turned and walked away.

I found my aunt talking to Pastor Joe. She looked furious. I stood a few feet away from her, afraid that I was about to be on the receiving end of her wrath. She abruptly ended her conversation with Pastor Joe, and her angry gaze settled upon me. Without a word, she yanked my arm and started dragging me towards the car.

"Did you tell Pastor Joe that my house was haunted?" she asked once we were out of earshot from the rest of the congregation.

"No," I replied. Saying that something was spooky was not the same as saying that it was haunted, I told myself.

"Do you know how much the resale value of a house could go down if people thought that it was haunted?" she asked.

"No. I'm sorry," I replied. I got into the car and held my purse tightly to my chest as if it could protect me from my aunt.

"Ahhhhh!" Aunt Rose screamed. "What is that?" she said as she pointed to my purse. "Is that blood? Is your purse bleeding?" she exclaimed in horror.

I lifted my purse up, and I could see strawberry jelly leaking out from the seams. "It's just jelly from my donuts," I replied as I licked it up before it could drip onto my dress. A look of revulsion crossed my aunt's face.

"Try not to ruin my car," she said as she started to drive home.

"Sorry," I said again, but she was not finished chastising me.

"Because of what you said, Pastor Joe is coming over today to do a house blessing," Aunt Rose said, incensed. I didn't think that a house blessing was a bad thing, but I decided to keep my opinion to myself. No matter what I said or did, it always seemed to be wrong.

I spent the next few hours hiding in my room from Aunt Rose. I was relieved when the doorbell rang. I went downstairs to open the door, but Aunt Rose was already down there letting Pastor Joe in.

"Hello, Rose and Lauren. My goodness, this is such an impressive home," Pastor Joe said as he glanced around the foyer.

"Thank you. I think it's quite beautiful," Aunt Rose added. Beautiful was not the word that I would have used to describe the place. Poopsie ran toward Pastor Joe and barked furiously.

"What a cute little dog," Pastor Joe said as he leaned forward to pet Poopsie. She bared her teeth and snapped at him. He quickly drew his hand back before she could bite him.

"Oh, Poopsie," Aunt Rose said as she scooped up the dog. "Did Pastor Joe scare you?" The dog could do no wrong. There was an awkward pause before Pastor Joe finally spoke.

"It's getting late. I should probably get started on the house blessing."

"Is there anything that I need to do?" Aunt Rose asked.

"If you could just walk me through the entire house, I would like to say a prayer in each room. You can silently pray with me."

"All right. This is the foyer, and through here is the dining room," Aunt Rose replied. Aunt Rose continued to lead Pastor Joe through each room on the main level. He would hold up his cross and say a special prayer each time. They were about to go upstairs when I felt an icy chill. The darkness that pervaded the house had returned, and I could sense evil waiting in the shadows upstairs. I hesitated to follow them.

"Aren't you coming up?" Aunt Rose asked.

"No. I think I'll wait down here with Poopsie," I replied. The sun was starting to set, and once darkness came, the hauntings would start again. Aunt Rose and Pastor Joe were at the top of the stairs when there was a deafening bang. It startled everyone.

"It's just the door to Lauren's room. It must have slammed shut from the wind," Aunt Rose explained. She went over to try to open it, but it wouldn't budge. "It must be stuck."

"Let me try," Pastor Joe offered. He tried with all his strength, but it still wouldn't open. "That's all right. I'll just bless the other rooms," Pastor Joe replied. I could hear them going through the upstairs bedrooms as I waited patiently in the foyer. Pastor Joe finally finished his blessings, and they both headed down the stairs. A moment later, there was the sound of a door slowly creaking open behind them. Pastor Joe paused to look back. The door to my bedroom had opened on its own, and you could hear the faint sound of footsteps coming toward them. Suddenly, Pastor Joe went flying down the stairs. A startled scream escaped from him before he landed on Aunt Rose and knocked her to the ground. They both laid there on the foyer floor in shock. Aunt Rose's dress had flipped up over her head, and her underwear, covered in tiny hearts, was showing. I tried not to laugh.

"Are you OK?" I asked. The sound of a child's laughter echoed through the house. Aunt Rose and Pastor Joe both looked up at me. I shrugged my shoulders. "It's not me," I replied, relieved that I hadn't laughed out loud at Aunt Rose's underwear. I looked up at the stairs where the laughter was coming from, and I could see the little girl standing there with her doll. A malevolent smile spread across her face, and I took a step back in horror.

"I'm so sorry. I must have tripped," Pastor Joe said as he scrambled up from the floor. He looked back at the top of the stairs and stood there motionless for the longest time. I could see him start to tremble.

"You can see her, can't you?" I whispered to Pastor Joe. He turned to look at me. All the color had drained from his face. He averted his eyes away from me and looked down at Aunt Rose lying on the floor.

"Are you all right?" he asked Aunt Rose as he tried to help her up. Aunt Rose tried to pull her dress down and regain some of her composure.

"I'm fine," she said as she slapped his hand away angrily.

"It's getting late. I should be going," Pastor Joe said as he started to run toward the front door. He was in such a hurry that he didn't see Poopsie's accident in the foyer, and he stepped directly on top of the pile of poop. "Oh, dear," he mumbled as he flung the front door open. I followed him to ask him if he had seen the little girl, but he was already halfway down the walkway. I could see him dragging his foot on the front lawn trying to get the offending material off his shoe. There was a loud piercing scream from a raven nearby before it swooped down and tried to claw his balding head. The pastor screamed and then sprinted to his car. I could hear the peeling of his tires as he drove away. At least you can go home, I thought to myself before I closed the front door. Aunt Rose picked up Poopsie who seemed upset by the whole incident.

"Oh, my poor little Poopsie. Did Pastor Joe scare you? He did, didn't he. He scared the poop right out of you," she said as she comforted the dog. "Lauren, please clean up this mess. I have to get ready for my date tonight."

"You have a date?" I said, panicked. "You're going to leave me alone by myself?"

"Yes. I told you about this date several days ago. Besides, you're a big girl."

"What about dinner?" I asked.

"Oh, I forgot you had to eat dinner. There are some frozen dinners in the freezer," she replied as I followed her into the kitchen. I opened the refrigerator and found some flour tortillas and cheese. I sliced the cheese and folded it into a tortilla and put it in the microwave.

"What are you making?" Aunt Rose asked.

"Cheese quesadillas," I replied. The microwave beeped, and I took the plate out and cut the quesadillas into slices. Aunt Rose took a slice.

"This is quite good," she replied as she took another slice.

"Thanks," I said as I hastily grabbed the last piece before Aunt Rose could eat it. "Who are you going out with tonight?" I asked in between bites.

"His name is Melvin. He works at the bank," she said with little excitement in her voice. "I'm going to go get ready. Don't forget to clean up the mess in the entry," she said as she left the room. Poopsie stayed in the kitchen with me. She stared at the last bite of my quesadilla.

"I guess we can share," I said as I fed it to her. I still had a purse full of donuts upstairs anyways. I went to find the paper towels and cleaning supplies. I was busy cleaning the floor when the doorbell rang.

"Can you get that, Little Quack Quack? I'm not ready yet," Aunt Rose yelled from upstairs.

"Sure," I said as I opened the door. A small, middle aged man with dark hair and dark eyes stood on the front door step.

"Hello, I'm Melvin. You must be Rose's niece. It's so nice to meet you," he said as he reached out to shake my hand.

"Come in. Aunt Rose isn't ready yet," I said as I stepped back to let him inside. He was holding a bouquet of flowers, and he looked nervous. Sweat was starting to bead on his forehead. When he tried to wipe it away, his hair went sliding back on his head. "Oh my gosh!" I gasped.

"What?" he asked.

"Your hair is trying to run away from you," I exclaimed.

"Oh," he said as his face turned bright red. He went to the mirror hanging above the entry table and pulled his hair back into place. He picked out a yellow daisy from the flower arrangement. "Here is a flower for you. Thank you for helping me." He seemed nice, and for a moment I thought about telling him to run as fast as he could away from Aunt Rose, but she had started to come down the stairs. Besides, if his hair was smart enough to run away, he would be too.

"It's so nice to finally meet you, Rose. These are for you," Melvin said as he handed her the bouquet. Aunt Rose seemed indifferent to the flowers and handed them to me.

"Thanks. You can put these in water," she said. "Well, I'm starving. I haven't eaten anything today. I hope that we're going somewhere with good food."

"Yes. I have reservations at one of the best restaurants in town," Melvin proclaimed. "I guess we should get going. It was nice meeting you," he said as he smiled at me.

"Be good, Little Quack Quack," Aunt Rose said before they both walked out the front door. I stood there staring at the closed door for a minute, unsure of what to do next. The phone rang loudly, and it startled me. I walked into the kitchen and warily picked up the phone. I was afraid of who might be on the other end.

"Hello," I whispered. I could hear static on the other end.

"Lauren, is that you?" the voice asked.

"Mom?"

"Yes, Pumpkin. It's me. How are you? I've missed you," Mom said warmly. I couldn't help myself. I started to cry.

"Mom, it's been so awful. The house is haunted by an evil little girl and a lady who plays the organ at night," I sobbed.

"Are you all right? No one has hurt you, have they?" she said, concerned.

"No, not really, but I'm sure that Aunt Rose's cooking is going to kill me," I replied dramatically.

"I'm so sorry. I know that she's not the best cook, but I should be coming home soon. Where is Rose? Can I talk to her?"

"She's on a date with someone named Melvin," I replied.

"She left you all alone?" Mom asked, surprised.

"She said I was a big girl."

"She shouldn't have done that. Should I call someone to come over and stay with you?" she said, concerned.

"No. Aunt Rose has done this before, and I was fine," I replied. Besides, no one could protect me from the ghosts.

"Make sure all the doors and windows are locked," she cautioned.

"I will," I promised.

"Now, what were you saying about a little girl and a woman playing the organ?" she asked, confused.

"Mrs. Harrison said that the lady who plays the organ at night is one of the original owners of the house. Her husband and son died in an accident, and I don't think that she's moved on."

"I hope that Mrs. Harrison isn't telling you scary stories again," Mom replied. She seemed upset. Mom had seen a ghost before, but she still had trouble believing in them.

"I saw the lady and heard the organ music before Mrs. Harrison even told me the story," I said defensively. "You believe me, don't you?"

She hesitated before she answered. "Yes, Pumpkin. I believe you."

"I also saw a little girl in the house. I think she might be Arabella Morgan. Did you know the Morgans?" I asked.

"I saw them in church, but they weren't very friendly with anyone. Mr. Morgan died from a heart attack quite a few years ago."

"What happened to Arabella?"

"I remember that Arabella got sick, and the entire congregation was praying for her."

"What was wrong with her?"

"I don't remember. I thought that she had leukemia or some kind of cancer, but I'm not sure. When she was no longer on the prayer list, I just assumed that she had passed away. Her mother looked so devastated that I didn't have the heart to ask her what happened. She sold the house shortly after that."

"I think that the little girl's spirit is still in the house. Pastor Joe came to bless the house today, and the door to Arabella's bedroom slammed shut. Pastor Joe couldn't get it open so he just left it alone, but once he finished the house blessing and was walking down the stairs, the bedroom door opened all by its self. Then Pastor Joe fell down the stairs. He knocked Aunt Rose to the ground, and you could hear a child laughing after it happened."

"That's terrible. They didn't get hurt, did they?" Mom asked.

"I don't think so. Aunt Rose's dress flipped up, and you could see her underwear. Then Pastor

Joe tried to run out of the house, but he stepped in a pile of poop," I said as I giggled. Mom laughed too.

"I don't think he'll be visiting Rose anytime soon. As long as you're all right, that's all I care about."

"I'm better now that I got to talk to you." Mom had believed me, and that was all that mattered. I also had John, and he was confident that we could figure everything out. "How is Grandma?"

"She's doing much better. I took her to the doctor's today, and they said that her arm is healing nicely. She's asleep right now. If all goes well, I should be coming home soon."

"I can't wait. I miss your cooking, I miss Susie, I miss my bedroom, but mostly I just miss you," I replied.

"You're going to make me cry," Mom said tearfully. "I miss and love you more than you can imagine. I'll call you tomorrow. Good night, Pumpkin."

"Good night, Mom," I said before I hung up the phone. I waited in the kitchen with Poopsie for a few minutes. I was afraid to go upstairs. My stomach growled loudly, and I remembered the donuts that I had stashed away in my bedroom. It was enough motivation to go up there. As I approached the bottom of the stairs, I waited and listened for any ghosts that might be lurking around. The sound of silence was deafening. I finally held my breath as I walked up the stairs. The floor boards creaked under my feet. There were no lights on upstairs, and I peered around each dark corner in fear. My heart raced as my imagination ran wild. I reached inside my bedroom and flipped on the light switch. I expected to jump back in horror, but everything in my room was just as I had left it. I decided the best option was to sleep in my bedroom with all the lights on. There was no way that Aunt Rose would let me sleep with her again, and sleeping downstairs wasn't safe anymore. I quickly found a pair of pajamas and put them on. I took my purse full of donuts and crawled into bed. I slowly savored every bite of delicious, sugary dough. When my stomach was finally full, I laid my head on my pillow and fell asleep a few minutes later.

When I woke up, I was in a dark cramped room filled with boxes. The ceilings were low, and there were cobwebs everywhere. I could hear haunting organ music playing below. I wasn't sure if I was dreaming or if I had sleep walked up to the attic. I had to find a way out. There was a small window, and the curtain that hung above it had been pulled back as if someone had been looking outside. A small sliver of moonlight shined through the window, and I could see a door on the opposite side of the room. I carefully walked around the stacks of boxes and old furniture and reached for the door knob. It was locked. I tugged and I pulled, but it was locked from the outside. I heard something scurry into the corner, and I hoped that it was a mouse and not someone hiding in the attic with me.

"Aunt Rose, can you help me? I can't get out!" I yelled. Despite the cold night air, sweat began to pour down my forehead. "Hello? Is anyone out there?" I yelled as I banged on the door. I began to panic. "Please, can someone help me?" I thought I heard someone coming up the stairs, and I stopped banging on the door to listen. The stairs creaked louder as someone approached.

A child's voice whispered from behind me, "He's coming. Hurry, you have to hide." The frightened voice seemed to be coming from the back of the room. I turned to look, but it was too dark to see if anyone was there. I could hear the footsteps grow louder as they approached the door. A shadow appeared under the door. A sense of dread came over me, and I took a step back, afraid of whoever might be standing there.

"You've been a very bad girl, and I have to punish you now," a male voice said angrily through the door. I recoiled in horror. It wasn't Aunt Rose. There was a man standing behind the door, and he wanted to hurt me. For a moment I stood there, paralyzed in fear as I heard a key being inserted into the lock.

"Hurry, run and hide," a childlike voice whispered behind me. I could feel the child's breath on my neck, but when I turned to look, no one was there. On shaky legs, I stumbled around until I reached the farthest corner of the attic and hid behind some boxes. The door opened, and I could hear footsteps as the man entered the room. I quietly peeked from behind the boxes to see who was there. Light coming from the open doorway illuminated the man from behind, and his ghostly white face glowed in the dark. It was the old man that I had seen die so many times at the bottom of the stairs. He looked enraged, and he was carrying a belt in his hands. He glanced at the corner where I was hiding, and I quickly scooted backwards before he could see me. My heart was pounding wildly, and I prayed that he hadn't seen me.

"Where are you hiding?" he demanded. "How dare you leave your clothes on the floor and eat food in your bed. You know that you're not supposed to do that. You've been a very bad girl, and now I have to punish you," he threatened loudly. He accidently banged his foot on one of the boxes and let out a few swear words. I thought about running out the open door, but he would catch me before I could get out. He started moving toward the corner of the attic where I was hiding in. Fear gripped me, and I bit my lip to keep from crying out. I started to shake violently as I heard him get closer and closer to my hiding spot. I crawled as far as I could into the corner and sat on something hard. I pulled it out from underneath me. It was a doll. I held it tightly to my chest as if it could protect me from what was coming. Silent tears began to roll down my face.

"Come out right now!" the man yelled. A small gasp escaped from my mouth, and I was afraid that I had given away my hiding spot. He stopped for a moment, and I was sure that he had heard me. I silently prayed for help. A moment later, I could hear footsteps again as he continued his systematic search of the attic. He was getting closer. There was no way out. Just a few more steps and he would see me. I turned my face and body toward the wall so that I wouldn't have to see what would happen next when he found me. There were several large spider webs in the corner, and I knocked them when I moved closer to the wall. I watched in sheer terror as several spiders fell onto my body. I felt their tiny legs crawling up my arms. I tried in vain to remain silent, but one of the spiders crawled across my face. I let out a bloodcurdling scream as I swatted violently at my arms and face.

Suddenly, I was blinded by a bright light. As my eyes finally adjusted and I looked around, I realized that I was in my bedroom again. Sunlight was flooding in through the window. All the lights were on, and ants were crawling all over my bed and pajamas, enjoying the tiny donut crumbs that I had left behind. I jumped out of bed and ripped off my pajamas. I swatted at the last few ants left on my arms and vowed never to eat food in my bed ever again. It was just a dream, I told myself, but as I looked down at my discarded pajamas, I could see that they were covered in dust and cobwebs.

Chapter 13

I hurriedly dressed and went downstairs to breakfast. I found the box of cereal and got out a bowl. My heart was still pounding, and my hands were shaking while I tried to pour milk into my cereal. It was just a dream, I reassured myself again. Aunt Rose came into the kitchen and poured herself a cup of coffee.

"Good morning, Little Quack Quack. Are you all right?" she asked as she looked at me more closely.

"I'm fine. I just had a bad dream," I replied. There was nothing that she could do to help me. "How was your date?" I asked as I ate my breakfast.

"It was nice, I guess. Melvin, he's...not very exciting," Aunt Rose replied. "And he's just so small." She sounded disappointed. Melvin was average height, but I could see how he would seem small in comparison to Aunt Rose.

"So you're not going to go out with him again?" I asked.

"No. He still wants to go out again. I should probably give him another chance," she replied. I felt bad for both of them.

"I better go to school now," I said as I got up to get my backpack.

Aunt Rose glanced up at me. "Did you even brush your hair?"

"No," I said guiltily as I tried to smooth the tangled mess with my fingers. "My mom usually braids my hair. Do you know how to do a French braid?" I asked.

"I can do regular braids," Aunt Rose said enthusiastically. "I'll be right back." She ran upstairs to get her hair brush and then proceeded to try to braid my hair. It took every ounce of will power not to scream from the pain that she was inflicting on me.

"I really have to go soon or I'll be late for school," I said as I tried to get away.

"One more minute," she insisted. I was relieved when she finally finished.

"I have to stay late after school today to work on a project with John. I'll be home before five," I said before I ran out the door.

"That's fine. I have to show a client a few houses. I won't be home until six. Don't forget your lunch," Aunt Rose said as she handed me a brown bag filled with something inedible in it. I ran all the way to school and arrived a few minutes early. I was excited. Today was the day that John and I would talk to Mrs. Morgan. It wouldn't be long before Arabella was reunited with her mother. Tommy came and sat down behind me in his desk.

"Did you get electrocuted?" he snickered as he pointed at my hair.

"I look beautiful, Tommy," I replied confidently. I hadn't looked in the mirror, but I didn't think that anyone could ruin a braid. I nonchalantly reached up to feel my hair. Pieces of hair were poking out everywhere, and it felt like the braids were projecting out at odd angles. I would have to check it out in the bathroom mirror during lunch, but I was definitely feeling less confident. Miss Sullivan came into the room and immediately started in on a history lesson. The lessons seemed to go by slowly before the bell finally rang for lunch.

"Lauren, can I talk to you?" Miss Sullivan asked as everyone left to go to lunch.

"Did I do something wrong?" I asked worriedly.

"No. I was just wondering if Rose did your hair today."

"Yes, she did," I said, perplexed. Why did she want to know about my hair?

"Would you like me to fix it for you?" she asked sympathetically. It must have looked worse than I thought.

"Yes, please," I replied, grateful for her kindness. She began to undo the hideous braids. Then she took a brush out of her purse and gently brushed out all the tangles.

"I'm sorry my hair is so messy," I replied, ashamed.

"It's not messy. It's perfect. If I had a little girl, I would want her to be just like you," she replied as she finished smoothing out my hair. "There, it's done. You look beautiful."

"Thanks, Miss Sullivan," I replied as I gave her a big hug. "You're the best teacher ever."

"Thank you, Lauren. You should go eat your lunch before the bell rings," she replied. I went to my locker and pulled out the brown bag. I found a small can of weenies and a celery stick. It was worse than I thought. I ate the celery and opened the can of sausages. They were floating in some kind of clear congealed fat. It made me lose my appetite. I threw the rest of my lunch into the trash as the bell rang and went back to my classroom. The rest of the day went by quickly, and I stood anxiously at the front of the school waiting for John to get out. I was relieved when he found me.

"Did your mom say that it would be OK if we went to the old folks' home?" I asked as soon as I saw him.

"Yes. She said that she'd pick me up at your aunt's house at five o'clock." He started to walk in the direction of the Oakdale Convalescent Hospital. I walked faster to try and keep up with him. I started to get nervous the closer that we got to our destination.

"Pastor Joe said that Sylvia Morgan was losing her memory. What if she doesn't remember Arabella?" I asked worriedly.

"She doesn't have to remember Arabella. Arabella will remember her. All we have to do is get her to your aunt's house," John reassured me. I tried to believe him, but I couldn't shake the sense of foreboding that had come over me.

"Have you seen Arabella again?" John asked. I told him the story about Pastor Joe coming over for the house blessing and stepping in a pile of poop. We both laughed, and I felt calmer as we arrived in front of an old three story building. It looked more like a college dorm than a hospital. There was an older lady sitting at a desk.

"I was wondering if we could visit Mrs. Sylvia Morgan. Pastor Joe said that she was staying here," John said as he flashed his brightest smile. The lady smiled back at him.

"What a sweet boy you are. I don't think Sylvia has had a single visitor since she's been here. She's in room 108. Just sign in right here," she said as she handed us a book. We both signed our names and walked down a hall to her room. My palms were sweaty, and I wiped them on my pants. The door to room 108 was open. There was a frail older woman sitting in a chair by the window. Her long, scraggly gray hair fell around her face and shoulders. She had a thin blanket pulled around her bony shoulders. John knocked on the door.

"Hi, Mrs. Morgan. I'm John, and this is Lauren," he said as he pointed at me. "Is it OK if we come in?" he asked. She just continued to stare out the window. John motioned for me to follow him into the room, and he pulled out a chair for me to sit in. The movement caught her attention, and she turned towards me. There was a demented look in her faded blue eyes. A ghoulish smile spread across her face as she reached out with her bony fingers and touched my face. I tried not to flinch, but she frightened me. With her long, hooked nose and yellow teeth, she reminded me of a wicked witch.

"You look so much like my Arabella," she said as she started to stroke my hair. I wanted to scream and run out of the room.

"What happened to Arabella?" John asked. Sylvia Morgan's hand fell away from my hair, and a sorrowful look crossed her face.

"Harold and I had wanted a child for so long. We tried so hard to be good to her, but she was such a difficult child. She would always leave her toys out and her dirty clothes on the floor. She would spill her drinks on the carpet, and I even caught her eating food in her bedroom. She had to be punished, you know. Harold would hit her with his belt or lock her in the attic. It didn't help though, and when she found the box of papers in the attic, she became even worse." Sylvia Morgan looked outside the window again.

"What box of papers?" I asked. She looked back at me with her crazed eyes.

"The papers that said that Arabella was adopted," she replied.

"She was adopted? Who was her mother?" I asked, desperate to find out.

"I don't know. It was a closed adoption. I only know that her birth mother lived here in Bozeman and that she had just graduated from high school. After Arabella found out about her adoption, she became so angry. She was convinced that Harold and I had stolen her from her mother. I tried to explain to her that her birth mother never wanted her, but she didn't believe me. She just became more angry and violent. After Harold died, I couldn't control her anymore. She was very sick, you know. I sent her to a special hospital in Billings. I was hoping that she would get better, but she never did. It was too late. It was just too late." A blank look crossed her face, and she turned to stare out the window again. Several minutes passed in silence.

"We should go," I said to John. Before I could get up from my chair, Sylvia Morgan turned around and grabbed my arm with her bony fingers. She looked ominous as her thin hair whipped around her face, and she stared at me with intense hatred.

"Arabella, what are you doing here?" she yelled.

"No. I'm not Arabella. I'm Lauren," I winced as I tried to pull my arm away.

"How dare you lie to me, Arabella," she said furiously. "You're an evil child. You killed him, didn't you? You killed my Harold."

"No. I didn't kill anyone," I cried as I struggled to pull away. I looked at John. He looked terrified.

"I'll go get help," he said as he ran out of the room.

"I know that you pushed Harold down the stairs. You caused him to have a heart attack. You're a murderer," she screamed.

"No. I didn't do anything," I cried.

"Stop lying. You're a murderer," she yelled. She paused for a moment. "Why have you come back?" she asked suspiciously. "Are you here to kill me too?" She immediately released my arm at the thought that I might hurt her. I stumbled backwards and knocked the chair over in my haste to get away. "Nurse, nurse," Sylvia screamed. "Stop her. She's going to kill me." As I reached the door, John arrived with a nurse and a doctor.

"Both of you please leave," the doctor ordered as the male nurse forcefully restrained Sylvia.

"Stop her. She's a murderer. You have to stop her. She's come here to kill me," I could hear Sylvia Morgan screaming as John and I ran down the hall and out of the hospital. The moment I stepped out onto the sidewalk, I burst into tears. It was too much, and John looked uncomfortable as I sobbed uncontrollably.

"It's OK, Lauren. We can still find Arabella's birth mother and help her to move on," John said as he patted me awkwardly on my back.

"No, we can't. Besides that, Arabella is a murderer."

"I don't believe that crazy old lady. Harold Morgan died from a heart attack. Pastor Joe didn't die when he was pushed down the stairs, did he?" John added.

"No," I replied in between sobs.

"I bet the adoption papers are still in the attic, and if we find them, maybe it will say who Arabella's birth parents were."

"You think so?" I asked, unsure.

"I'm positive," John replied optimistically. "And guess what else I found while I was at the hospital?"

"What?" I asked as I watched John reach into his backpack.

"One of the nurses gave me these," he said as he pulled out some muffins. "I know that they're muffins for old people, but they could still be good. Would you like one?" John offered. After eating just a meager celery stick at lunch, I was starving.

"OK," I said as I wiped my nose on my sleeve and picked out one of the muffins. I took a bite. It was a surprisingly delicious bran muffin with raisins and a hint of molasses. "Thanks, John. You're a good friend."

"I know," he smiled. We walked silently back to my aunt's house, eating our muffins. It was late afternoon by the time I unlocked the front door with the key that my aunt had given me.

"Should we go up into the attic to try to find the adoption papers?" I asked.

"I don't know. It's getting late. Do you think that there are ghosts up there right now?" John replied as he glanced up at the top of the staircase.

"I don't see any right now, but it's going to get dark soon, and that's when they usually come out," I replied honestly.

"Oh, my gosh! Do you smell that foul odor? Do you think it's coming from something evil in the house?" John said as he plugged his nose.

"Sorry. That was me. It must have been the bran muffins," I replied as I tried to wave my hand back and forth to clear the air. We both laughed.

"Maybe we can sit outside and wait for my mom. She should be here soon," John suggested.

"Sure," I said as we went out the front door and sat on one of the steps. We watched the sunset as we talked about school. John's mom finally came, and he waved goodbye to me as he got into the car. I was sad to see him go. Aunt Rose arrived just as John was leaving.

"Did you finish the project that you were working on with John?" Aunt Rose asked.

"No. John is going to come back tomorrow," I replied.

"That's fine. I'm going to go start dinner. Have you finished all your homework?" she asked.

"No. I'll go work on it right now."

"I'll call you when dinner is ready," Aunt Rose replied as she went into the kitchen. I went upstairs to my bedroom and worked on some math homework. An hour passed before I heard my aunt calling me to come down for dinner.

"Why don't you set the table," Aunt Rose suggested as I walked into the kitchen.

"OK," I replied as I went to take out some plates from the cabinet.

"What happened to the braids that I gave you this morning?" Aunt Rose asked as I was setting the table for dinner.

"Tommy told me that I looked like I had been electrocuted, so my teacher helped me take them out," I replied.

"How dare that little boy make fun of your braids. I'll walk you to school tomorrow, and you just point him out and I'll beat him up for you," she threatened as she shook her fists.

"No, Aunt Rose. That would be wrong. Didn't you hear the sermon at church on Sunday? You're supposed to love your enemies and pray for them," I urged.

"I couldn't hear the sermon over Mrs. Harrison's snoring."

"She was pretty loud," I agreed. "What's for dinner?" I asked, trying to change the subject. I hoped that I had convinced her because I was pretty sure that I would be thrown out of school if someone thought that I had hired Aunt Rose to beat up Tommy for me.

"I'm making a tuna casserole and boiled cabbage. They're low calorie dishes that are supposed to help me lose weight," she replied as she stirred a pot on the stove. She must have seen the look of disgust on my face because she added, "Don't worry, Little Quack Quack. I also made some brownies and hot cocoa for you." I perked up at the thought of brownies. Aunt Rose put the dishes on the table. "I know, I won't forget to say grace," Aunt Rose said as we both sat down at the table. She folded her hands and said, "Lord, my tummy is a-rumbling, so let's stop this mumbling, and let's eat. Amen."

It wasn't grace that I had heard before, but I guess it counted. Aunt Rose spooned some boiled cabbage and tuna casserole onto my plate. It smelled like stinky feet and cat food. I took a few small bites of each dish. It tasted worse than it smelled. I could see why you would lose weight on it. I looked up, and I could see that Aunt Rose was just moving the food around on her plate.

"How is it?" she asked.

"Good," I lied. "I'm getting kind of full. Do you think I could have dessert now?"

"Of course," she said as she got up to get the brownies. She came back with a cup of hot cocoa and a plate of brownies. There was something oily floating on top of the hot cocoa.

"Why is the hot cocoa greasy?" I asked.

"I put butter in it to make it creamier," she replied.

I took a sip. It was disgusting. Only Aunt Rose could ruin hot cocoa. I looked at the plate of brownies. The frosting had tiny beads of moisture on it as if it had been sweating. The brownie hadn't cooked all the way through and dark liquid was leaking out around it. It reminded me of the poop that I had cleaned up the other day. I heard a scratching sound on the floor, and when I looked down, I saw Poopsie scooting her bottom across the floor. I lost what was left of my appetite.

"I'm tired today. I should probably go to bed early," I said as I picked up my plates and dumped what was left in the trash before Aunt Rose could say anything.

"Since I did all the cooking, you'll have to do all the dishes before you can go to bed," Aunt Rose said as she got up and left the kitchen and the mess that went with it.

I started putting all the food away. I offered Poopsie some of the tuna casserole, but she stuck her nose up at it and walked away. It took me an hour before the kitchen was finally clean. As I pushed the start button on the dishwasher, I heard the rumble of thunder in the distance, and it scared me. Poopsie whined.

"It's all right girl. It's just a storm," I reassured her as I patted her head. She went over and curled up on her bed. "I guess it's time for me to go to bed too," I said as I reluctantly headed upstairs. The hallway was dark except for the light coming from Aunt Rose's room. I silently crept to my room and peeked inside to make sure that no one was there. It was too dark to see anything. Suddenly, there was a flash of lightning outside my bedroom window. In the flickering of the light, I could see the silhouette of a little girl standing there by the window. The room was plunged back into darkness again, and the clap of thunder that followed was so violent that it shook the floor beneath my feet. I turned to run. I could hear the sound of footsteps behind me, but I refused to look back. I flung the door to my aunt's room open and ran inside.

"Help me, there's someone in my room," I yelled as I made a flying leap into Aunt Rose's bed. A ghostly figure lying in the bed stared back at me. Her corpselike face was bone white and covered in tiny cracks and fissures. As she opened her mouth to speak, more cracks seem to form on her face and pieces of her skin flaked off onto to the bed.

"Aaahhhhh!" I screamed as I jumped backwards off the bed in horror.

"Lauren, what is wrong with you?" the ghostly face asked me. It was Aunt Rose. She was wearing some kind of awful face cream.

"There's a ghost in my room," I said, terrified.

"There is no such thing as ghosts," Aunt Rose replied adamantly.

"Can you at least check my bedroom for me?" I said as I trembled.

"Fine," Aunt Rose replied. She looked irritated as she pulled her covers off and marched over to my room. I followed closely behind her. She walked into my room and switched the light on.

"There," she said as she pointed at the rocking chair. "You probably saw the sweater draped around the back of the chair and thought it was a person." It looked nothing like a person to me.

"Can you check the closet too?" I asked. She went over and opened the door.

"See, there's nothing in there. Now go to bed," she said as she started to walk out of the room. There was another loud clap of thunder, and I jumped.

"Can I sleep with you tonight? Please," I begged.

"The best way to get rid of your fears is to face them. Now go to bed," Aunt Rose said firmly as she walked out of the room and shut the door behind her.

I quickly turned on the rest of the lights in the bedroom. Then I took out a flashlight from one of the drawers that I had put there in case the power went out again. Nothing bad ever happens in the dark, I told myself. I put my pajamas on and grabbed the flashlight and crawled into bed. My stomach growled. I was starving, and I regretted not eating the brownies even though they looked like poo. There was another flash of lightning followed by thunder that shook the entire house. I threw the covers over my head and turned on my flashlight. Nothing bad ever happens in the dark, I chanted over and over again. It seemed like hours before the storm started to calm down, and the sound of rain finally lulled me to sleep.

The deafening sound of thunder woke me from my slumber. It was pitch black under my covers. I felt around for my flashlight, but I couldn't find it. It must have fallen off the bed. I felt like I was suffocating under the heavy weight of my blankets and pulled them off of me. The room was dark. The electricity must have gone off because of the storm. As my eyes adjusted to the shadowy darkness, I could see that I was no longer in my canopy bed. There was no doll house or rocking chair, just a small bed in a narrow, sterile room. A flash of lightning temporarily lit up the room and I could see scratched onto the walls the words, *Where's my mommy?* written hundreds of times over the entire space. I jumped out of bed in fear. Where was I? The gloomy room was ice cold, and I thought about crawling back under the blankets until I heard a scratching noise coming from under the bed.

"Poopsie, is that you?" I asked as my voice quivered in fear. I knew that it wasn't her. She would never come upstairs, and even if she had, this was not my bedroom. Whatever was under the bed had started to crawl out. I took a few steps back in horror as I watched two arms reach out from under the bed. I stumbled back against the wall and inched along it, hoping to find a door to escape out of the room. The ghastly being moved on its hands and knees toward me. Long, matted hair covered its face, and the unearthly creature made noises that didn't sound human. A flash of lightning lit up the room for a moment, and the creature looked up and stared at me. Ferocious blue eyes seemed to burn a hole right through me.

"Where's my mommy?" she demanded. A scream escaped from me as I saw her move closer to me before the room was plunged into darkness again. I slid along the wall away from her and suddenly felt the cold metal door handle against my back. I fumbled with shaky hands to open the door as the scratching noise came closer. Sheer terror gripped me as the door handle slipped through my sweaty fingers. I used both hands to turn the knob, and as I opened the door, something grabbed my leg. I kicked with all my might and got away. I ran into a long dark hallway with doors on either side. A man in hospital scrubs appeared at one end of the hallway.

"Get back in your room right now," he yelled at me. I ran frantically in the opposite direction. He started to run after me. Arms seemed to reach out from the rooms along the hall and tried to grab me. Strange screams and sounds reverberated through the walls. I ran blindly through endless hallways and down stairs trying to find a way out. I could hear the storm raging outside. My heart was pounding, and my lungs began to burn. I ran down another set of stairs and through a door. As I opened it, I was blinded by a light, and it took me a moment to realize that I was in a hospital waiting area. I could see the exit door, and I made a dash for it.

"Stop her," a voice from behind me yelled. I ran as fast as I could through the doors and out into the storm. As I looked back, I could see a tall, gothic building with a crumbling stone exterior behind me. It looked more like a prison than a hospital with bars on the windows and depressing grey paint. A security guard ran out the doors toward me. I turned to run as fast as I could toward the cluster of pine trees on the edge of the property. I just have to make it to the trees, I told myself as rain pelted my face and body. My legs felt weak, and I could hear the guard gaining on me. It was too late. I would never make it before he caught up with me. I felt the man grab my arm, and I fell to the ground. I screamed and screamed until there was no more breath left in me.

"Stop screaming," a voice commanded. I woke suddenly and found my aunt shaking my arm. I looked around, and I was back in my room. "You were having a bad dream," she explained. Never in my life did I think I would be so happy to see Aunt Rose, but I was. "You're soaking wet. You must have sweated a lot with all those heavy blankets on you," she concluded. "You should go change."

"It was just a bad dream," I reassured myself.

"Of course, it was just a bad dream. You better hurry up or you'll be late for school," Aunt Rose added before she released my arm and walked out of the room.

"It was just a bad dream," I repeated again, but as I reached up and touched my damp hair, I just wasn't sure about anything anymore.

Chapter 14

I got dressed for school and went down and ate breakfast in silence. Aunt Rose was on the phone with a client. She waved goodbye to me as I went out the front door. It was a beautiful fall day. The sky looked bright blue against the mountains, and it was hard to feel afraid on such a majestic morning. I made it to school on time and was relieved that Tommy was absent today. I tried to concentrate on the lessons, but my mind kept wandering back to my nightmare from last night and all the horrible things that Sylvia Morgan had yelled at me yesterday. I was relieved when school finally ended, and I found John waiting for me at the front of the school.

"Are you ready to go?" John asked.

"Yeah," I replied as we started to walk toward my aunt's house.

"Did you see her again?" John asked with curiosity.

"I'm not sure. I thought that I saw a little girl in my bedroom last night, but Aunt Rose checked my room, and no one was there. Then I had a really bad dream."

"What was your dream about?" John asked.

"I actually had two weird dreams over the last couple of nights. In the first dream, I was locked in the attic, and an old man came in with a belt to punish me for being bad. I hid from him, and then when I woke up, I was in my bedroom." I left out the part about being covered in ants because I had eaten donuts in bed. "Then last night, I dreamed I was in a hospital and Arabella crawled out from under the bed and asked me where her mother was. I ran out of the room and down some stairs out of the building, but a guard grabbed my arm and pinned me to the ground. I screamed, and when I woke up, my aunt was shaking my arm and telling me to wake up. What do you think the dreams meant?"

"I think that Arabella is trying to communicate with you. Sylvia Morgan said that her husband used to lock Arabella up in the attic to punish her. Maybe Arabella is trying to show you what her life was really like because no one ever knew, and she wanted someone to know the truth."

"That makes sense. She must have had a really terrible life," I said as I remembered all the horrible things that had happened in my dreams. We walked up the driveway to the house, and I took out my key to open the front door. Our footsteps echoed in the entryway as we stepped inside. Even in the daylight, a dark presence seemed to pervade the house.

"Do you think it's safe to go up to the attic?" John asked as his voice quivered.

"I think so. I don't see or hear anything," I replied as I looked around.

"Do you know how to get to the attic?" John asked.

"No."

"There must be a door or a set of stairs leading up to it on the second floor. You should go first since you know the way upstairs," John suggested. I secretly thought that John wanted me to go first because he was afraid of what might be up there. I was just grateful that he was helping me, so I didn't say anything and started walking up the stairs. It was dark at the top of the stairs, and I hesitated for a moment.

"This is my bedroom," I said as I pointed to my room. We walked down the long hallway. "This is my aunt's bedroom and a guest bedroom." We had reached the end of the hallway. There was door that I had never opened before. "I don't know what's in here," I replied as I hesitantly reached for the door knob. I tried to open it, but it was stuck.

"Here, let me try," John offered. He pushed hard on the door until it finally opened. There was a set of wooden stairs that led up to a dark room. "Ladies first," John replied as he stepped back to let me go up first.

"No way," I said hastily. "You're just afraid to go up there," I blurted out.

"No. I was just trying to be a gentleman," he replied innocently, but the quiver in his voice gave him away. "Fine. I'll go first," he finally conceded.

The stairs creaked with each step that we took, and my heart began to race. We both stood at the top at the stairs and looked around. The curtain above the window had been pulled back as if someone had been looking out, and a small ray of light shined through the dirty pane of glass. I stared at the boxes and old furniture covered in dust and cobwebs. It was exactly like it had been in my dream.

"Why don't you look through the boxes at one end of the attic and I'll look through the boxes at the other end?" John suggested.

"No way. I'm sticking close to you," I insisted.

"OK, but it might take us a while," John replied. He seemed overwhelmed by the number of boxes.

"That's fine," I said as I started sorting through the boxes closest to us. Something scurried into the corner, and I jumped.

"It's probably just a mouse," John reassured me as he opened another box. I found dishes and old linens but no papers. The minutes turned into an hour, and I felt less hopeful with each box that I opened. I was dirty, and sweat was starting to pour down my forehead.

"It's really hot in here," I commented to John.

"I know. I'll go open the window," John said as he tried to maneuver around all the junk to get to the window. I felt a cold breeze, but when I looked up, John was still struggling to open the window.

The hair stood up on my arms, and fear began to well up inside me. Someone was here with us. I heard a slight movement in the corner, and when I turned to look, I could see something dark crouching behind a box.

"John?" I cried out in a panicked voice. A second later a small toy ball went flying across the room and hit John on the back of the head.

"Lauren, that wasn't very nice," John said as he turned around and gave me a dirty look.

"It wasn't me," I swore.

"Yes, it was," John replied as he went to retrieve the ball to throw it back at me. It had landed in a box nearby. As he pulled the ball out, he paused for a moment to look at something inside the box. He dropped the ball. "I found it, Lauren. I found the adoption papers," he declared happily. John picked up the box.

"Let's hurry and get out of here," I said nervously as I glanced in the corner again. I heard the sound of movement again, and I saw the little girl staring at me. Her eyes seemed to glow in the dark. For a moment, I was paralyzed with fear as she looked directly at me with a sinister smile on her face. She held me in some kind of trance, unable to look away or even move. She raised her hand toward me, beckoning me to come closer as if she had a secret to tell me. It was as if I had no control over my body as I took a step toward her. I silently commanded myself to stop, but I couldn't. I moved closer and closer. I tried to yell out to John, but only a silent gasp escaped from my mouth. I was so close now that if I reached my hand out to her, I could touch her. Her ghoulish smile widened as she leaned her head toward me and whispered, "There's something that I need to tell you."

"Are you OK?" John asked me. The moment he spoke, the spell was broken and the little girl was gone. I turned to run, not caring if John was behind me. I ran down the stairs at lightning speed, and I waited for John in the entry way.

"Thanks for leaving me behind," John said as he made his way down slowly with the box of papers.

"I'm sorry. I got scared. You didn't see her?"

"See what?" John asked. He obviously never saw what I had just seen hiding in the attic, and I wasn't going to tell him for fear that he wouldn't help me anymore. "Why don't we put the papers on the dining room table and go through them," John suggested.

"That's a good idea," I replied as I followed him into the dining room. He gave me half the papers to go through. A lot of it was legal mumbo jumbo that I didn't understand.

"I don't know what a lot of these words mean," I said, frustrated.

"Don't worry. We don't need to understand everything. All we have to do is find the birth certificate, and it should list the birth parents names," John replied.

"How do you know that?" I asked.

"I saw it in a movie."

"OK. That sounds easy enough," I said as I flipped through the papers. In between a few of the legal papers, I found a smaller, ornate piece of paper with the words "State of Montana, Certificate of Birth" written at the top. "I found it," I said excitedly, but my excitement was short-lived as I scanned the document. "I don't understand. It lists Sylvia Morgan and Harold Morgan as her parents."

"Let me see," John replied as I handed him the paper. "The state must have given a new birth certificate after the adoption. I bet the law firm or the adoption agency has the original certificate. Maybe we can call them and ask them about it. I found their addresses and phone numbers on some of the documents," John said as he shuffled the papers and pulled out the ones that he was looking for. "You can call the adoption agency and ask them what we need to do to find out who the birth parents are. You'll have to pretend that you're Arabella."

"I'm not very good at lying," I said reluctantly.

"You lie every time you say that you didn't fart when you really did," John argued.

"But that's not the same thing as saying that you're someone that you're really not," I replied.

"Then I guess we'll never find Arabella's birth parents," John said, frustrated.

"OK, I'll try," I replied as I got up to get the phone in the kitchen. John's guilt trip had worked. I sat back down at the dining room table and dialed the number on the paper that John had given me.

"New Dawn Adoption Agency. How can I help you?" a cheerful voice on the other end answered.

"Hi, my name is Arabella Morgan, and I'm trying to find my birth parents. Can you help me?" I asked.

"I'll certainly try. Are you over the age of eighteen?" she replied.

"Yes," I lied, unsure of Arabella's exact age.

"Then you can fill out an application online," she said as she spelled the name of the website out loud for me. "Someone will review your application and get back to you in a few weeks."

"A few weeks?" I said, surprised.

"These things take time," she said sympathetically.

"Oh," I said, disappointed.

"I'm sorry, sweetheart. I can at least look up your name to make sure that you're in our system," she offered.

"Thank you," I replied with new hope as I scrambled to find the birth certificate.

"Please spell your name and give me your date of birth."

"My first name is A-r-a-b-e-l-l-a, and my last name is M-o-r-g-a-n," I said as I spelled out the letters for her. "My birthday is September 19, 2000." I held my breath as I waited for her answer.

"I have good news and bad news. The good news is that you are in our system, but the bad news is that according to your birthdate, you're only sixteen. I'm sorry, sweetie. In two years you can fill out the application unless you can get your adoptive parents to sign a waiver allowing you to see your adoption papers sooner."

"No, I can't do that," I said, discouraged.

"I'm sorry that I couldn't help you more. It often takes people years to find their birth parents," she said compassionately.

"Thanks for trying to help me."

"You're welcome. Good luck, sweetie," she said as I heard a click on the other end. I put the phone down.

"What did she say?" John asked impatiently.

"You have to be 18 years old to put in an application for information on your birth parents, and Arabella would have been only sixteen this year. Do you think that you could call the law firm and see if they know anything?" I suggested as a last-ditch effort.

"I think that there is some kind of confidentiality rule where a lawyer can only talk to his client about a case. At least that's what I've seen on television shows." There was a knock at the door, and we both got up to see who was there.

"Your mom is here," I replied as I looked through the side window. John picked up his backpack and opened the door.

"Don't worry, Lauren. We'll figure out something," John said, but even he couldn't hide his discouragement.

"Bye," I said as I watched John get in the car. I felt depressed. Eating always made me feel better, so I headed to the kitchen to find something to eat. I was able to scrounge up a can of tomato soup and some bread and cheese. Mom had taught me how to make grill cheese sandwiches. I heard the front door open, and Aunt Rose came into the kitchen a minute later.

"It smells good in here. What are you making?" Aunt Rose asked.

"Tomato soup and grilled cheese sandwiches. I made some for you," I replied as I handed her a plate. I sat down beside her and started to eat.

"Thank you. This is good," she said in between mouthfuls. "I shouldn't eat so much. Melvin is taking me out to dinner tonight."

"You're going out again tonight?" I said anxiously. I was afraid to be alone.

"Yes. I told you that I was going to give him a second chance," she said as she wiped her hands on a napkin. The doorbell rang. "Oh, no. I lost track of time. He's already here. Hurry and answer the door. I'm just going to run up and change," Aunt Rose replied as she dashed out of the room. I walked over to the front door and opened it.

"Hi, Lauren. Is your aunt here?" Melvin asked. He had another bouquet of flowers for her.

"She's getting ready upstairs. She should be down soon," I replied as I opened the door wider to let him in.

"This is such a grand house. How do you like staying here?" he asked.

"It's awful. The house is haunted," I replied. I forgot that I wasn't supposed to say that. Aunt Rose was going to be mad at me.

"I heard rumors that it's haunted. I've always wanted to see a ghost," Melvin said wistfully. I was about to tell him that they were scary and he didn't really want to see one, but Aunt Rose started to come down the stairs.

"What's this about ghosts? Has Lauren been telling you that the house is haunted?" Aunt Rose asked as she gave me a stern look.

"No. It wasn't Lauren, it was me. I've just always had a fascination with haunted houses," Melvin replied. Aunt Rose turned and directed her angry stare at Melvin.

"This house is NOT HAUNTED!!!" she shouted at him. "I've lived here for over a month, and I haven't seen or heard anything unusual. I'd appreciate it if you would not spread any rumors or lies about my home."

"I'm very sorry. I meant no harm. Here, I brought you some flowers," he offered. I could see his hand shake as Aunt Rose just stood there staring daggers at him.

"I'll put these in water for you," I replied as I gently took the flowers from his hand. I appreciated that Melvin had taken the hit for me, but I was pretty sure that this would be their last date together. I was going to miss him. He was kind to me.

"You better be in bed before I get home," Aunt Rose yelled at me.

"I will be. I promise. Goodbye, Melvin."

"Goodbye, Lauren," Melvin said sadly as they both walked out the front door. I went back into the kitchen to finish my soup and sandwich. It seemed especially frigid in the house tonight, and I started to shiver. The food was cold, and it didn't taste as good anymore. I heard the front door open, and Poopsie ran out of the kitchen and started barking.

"Did you forget something, Aunt Rose?" I asked as I walked into the foyer. I stopped dead in my tracks. There was a large, older woman with frizzy, white hair wearing a vintage, lace dress. She was standing by the front door with her suitcase. I took a step back in fear.

"Who are you?" I asked. The older woman remained silent. "Are you alive or dead?" I whispered as I trembled.

"Oh, dear. I must look pretty bad if you can't tell the difference," she replied as she laughed. "I'm Rose's mother. You must be Lauren. I heard that my daughter had bought this big house, and I wanted to come and visit. I thought that I'd surprise her. I've been worried about her being all alone out here. Is Rose here?" she asked.

"She's out on a date," I replied.

"Oh, Rose is dating someone? Tell me all about him and don't leave out any of the good parts," she said gleefully. I liked her.

"His name is Melvin, and he works at the bank. I think he's nice."

"Is Rose in love with him?" she asked, hopeful.

"I don't think so. She said that he was too small and not very exciting," I replied.

"That's too bad, but don't worry. I think that I met her future husband on my trip over here," she exclaimed joyfully.

"Really? Who is he?" I asked. Her excitement was contagious, and it was nice to have someone to talk to.

"His name is David Applebottom," she replied, and I snickered when I heard his name. "He's going to be the head chef at a new restaurant that is opening up in town. He would be perfect for my Rose. I don't know if you noticed, but she can't cook very well."

"I've noticed," I replied.

"Not only does he love to cook, but he also loves to travel like my Rose does. He's a big, handsome young man, and I just know in my heart that they're soulmates. I gave him her phone number, and I hope that he calls her."

"I hope so too," I replied. Maybe he would make Aunt Rose happy, and she wouldn't be so angry at me all the time.

"It's getting late, and I'm afraid that I can't stay up any longer. Would it be all right if you showed me to one of the guest rooms?"

"Sure. There is one upstairs across from my bedroom," I replied as I started to walk up the stairs. She picked up her suitcase and followed me. I opened the door to her room.

"This is lovely. Thank you, Lauren. Good night. Sweet dreams," she wished me.

"Good night," I replied, but I hoped that I didn't have any dreams at all. I went to the bathroom and brushed my teeth. The pajamas that I wore last night were still on the floor, and I put them on. I crept over to my bedroom. The lights were off, and it was dark inside. I could hear the sound of something creaking back and forth inside my bedroom. "Hello, is someone there?" I asked. No one answered, but the rhythmic creaking continued. Maybe Aunt Rose had left the fan on in my bedroom. I finally got enough courage and reached my hand inside and tried to find the light switch. As I flipped it on, it illuminated the whole room. I looked over to where the sound of the creaking was coming from, and I could see the rocking chair moving back and forth on its own as if someone where sitting on it. A gasp escaped from me, and I ran over to the guest room. I barged in without knocking. Rose's mom was in her nightgown, lying in bed.

"Is everything all right?" she asked, concerned.

"Something scared me. Can I sleep with you?" I pleaded.

"Of course. My little Rose used to be afraid of the dark. I would always keep a night light on for her." I couldn't imagine Aunt Rose being afraid of anything.

"Can I keep a light on tonight too?" I asked.

"Sure. I'll turn on this bedside lamp for you. Now get some rest. Everything is going to be fine," she reassured me. She was such a nice, old lady. She was nothing like Aunt Rose, and I was so grateful that she was here. I climbed into the bed beside her and pulled the blankets up under my chin. I slept peacefully for the first night since I had arrived.

Sometime in the middle of the night, I heard organ music being played below. The notes sounded different this time. It wasn't the same mournful melody that was usually played over and over again. I had heard this tune before. It was a haunting rendition of the Wedding March. Maybe the lady in grey knew something that I didn't know. Maybe Aunt Rose would marry Mr. Applebottom. I smiled at the thought and eventually drifted back to sleep as the music played on and on.

Chapter 15

I woke up feeling great. I didn't have a single nightmare last night, and I had made a new friend. The organ music had played all night, but in a weird way, I had actually gotten used to it. I noticed that the other side of the bed was empty. I guess that Rose's mom had already gotten up. I heard that old people liked to get up early, but I was definitely not a morning person. I hurried to get dressed for school and went downstairs. Aunt Rose was just finishing up a conversation on the phone. I poured some cereal into a bowl.

"How are you doing, Little Quack Quack?" Aunt Rose asked as soon as she got off the phone.

"Good. Where's your mom?" I asked.

"Why would you think that my mom would be here?" she asked.

"She showed up last night. She said that she wanted to surprise you and that she had met your soulmate. His name is Mr. Applebottom, and she gave him your phone number," I replied. I was sure that Aunt Rose would be happy about the news.

"David Applebottom just called me. He's new in town, and he wants me to show him some properties today. You probably overheard the conversation," Aunt Rose replied matter-of-factly.

"No. Your mom told me about him last night. She probably went out to get some food because you don't have any," I said defensively.

"I don't know what kind of game you're playing, but there is no way that my mother was here," Aunt Rose said in an agitated voice.

"I'm not playing a game. I swear that she was here last night," I protested.

"She couldn't have been," Aunt Rose said sharply. "She died five years ago."

"No. That's not true. It's not true," I said, shocked. I pushed my chair back and ran upstairs to the guest bedroom. I would show Aunt Rose the suitcase that her mother had brought with her last night. Then she would have to believe me. I searched the entire room and even looked under the bed, but there was no suitcase. I glanced over at the bed, but it looked as if only one person had slept there last night. I sat down on the bed and cried. A few minutes later, I could hear Aunt Rose yelling that I was going to be late for school. I wiped my tears away and went downstairs. Aunt Rose looked visibly shaken and angry.

"We'll talk about this when you get home," she said as she crammed a lunch bag into my backpack and handed it to me. I grabbed my bag and ran out the door. It was a gloomy day, and it had started to sprinkle. It was probably a good thing because it hid the tears that were streaming down my face. By the time school started, I had stopped crying, but I still felt complete despair. I couldn't tell the living from the dead, and John and I had failed in finding Arabella's mother. Why couldn't I be like everyone else? I stared out the window at the grey sky and didn't even care that Tommy was throwing spit wads at me. The bell rang for lunch, but I didn't want to talk to anyone. I sat alone on a swing eating one of the diet protein bars that Aunt Rose had put in my lunch. A girl from the kindergarten class came and sat down on the swing next to me.

"Why are you so sad?" she asked. I couldn't tell her the real reason.

"I miss my mom," I replied truthfully.

"Where is she?" she asked as she started to swing back and forth. I could see her long, brown hair swaying in the wind.

"She had to go take care of Grandma for a while, but she's coming home soon."

"That's good. Mommies make everything better. And don't worry, you're going to find the other girl's mommy very soon," she said as she turned to smile at me. The comment startled me, and as I turned to look at her, I could see that one side of her face was burned beyond recognition. I jumped off the swing in horror and ran toward the school.

"Are you all right, Lauren?" Miss Sullivan asked as she stopped me in the school yard.

"Everything is fine," I hastily replied, but when I looked back, I could see that one of the swings continued to swing back and forth as if someone was still on it. Everything wasn't all right, and it never would be.

I could barely concentrate the rest of the day because I was so shaken up. As soon as the bell rang, I put my books in my backpack and headed for the library. I didn't want to go back to the haunted house and incur the wrath of my aunt. Besides, she usually didn't get back until after five. The library was my sanctuary. As soon as I walked in, Miss Gladys Peters greeted me at the front desk.

"Hello, Lauren. How are you?" she asked as she got up and started to walk over toward me. I couldn't help it. I started crying. "Oh, dear. What's wrong?" she asked as she wrapped her arms around me. I couldn't stop sobbing. Miss Peters just held me tighter and lovingly stroked my long, blond hair. "Are your mom and grandma all right?" she asked, concerned.

"They're fine," I replied in between sobs.

"Was Rose mean to you?" she asked.

"She's just as mean as she usually is," I replied. I couldn't tell her the real reason that I was upset.

"You know how much I love you and your mom. I consider you my family. You can tell me anything," she said. For a moment I thought about confiding in her, but Tommy walked into the library and saw me crying.

"Lauren is a crybaby," he taunted.

"Tommy, you apologize or I'll call security and have you escorted out," Miss Peters threatened. I appreciated her standing up for me.

"Sorry," he said unapologetically and ran up the stairs.

"Tommy Carson is a rotten little boy. Did you know that I've caught him several times picking his nose and wiping his dirty fingers in the library books? That's a criminal offense, defacing a library book like that," Miss Peters said indignantly. I had found some of the booger books in the library, but I didn't know that Tommy was the culprit. "Anyways, I'm sorry that you're so sad. How about if I take you out to dinner on Friday? I get off early that day."

"I would like that. I'll ask my aunt if it's OK," I replied. Miss Peters made me feel better, and I was looking forward to a decent meal.

"I have to go help someone check out a book. I'll see you on Friday," she replied as she walked back to her desk. I went upstairs and sat at a table. I was working on a history assignment when the old Native American man came and sat down at my table.

"You seem troubled," he said as he studied me.

"I met an old woman last night and a little girl today. I thought that they were alive, but they were really ghosts. Why can't I always tell the living from the dead?" I asked.

"It will get easier with time," he replied calmly.

"I don't want it to get easier. I want it to go away. Do you know how to make it go away?" I asked, upset. He just stared at me for the longest time. His eyes seemed to probe deep into my soul. For a moment I was hopeful that he could help me.

Instead he replied, "You are having trouble with one of the spirits." It was not an answer to my question at all. I felt hopeless again. Maybe he could at least help me with Arabella.

"Do you remember the angry, violent girl who wanted me to find her mother? I found out that she was adopted, but when I tried calling the adoption agency, they said that they couldn't give out any information for another two years. What should I do next to find her mother?" I asked. He paused as he contemplated what I had just said.

"If you are meant to find her mother, you will find her," he replied.

"That's not very helpful," I said, frustrated at all the old man's answers to my questions. "What happens if I never find her mother? Will she haunt me forever?" I asked, distressed.

"I do not know. In the meantime, you must show this spirit love. Love is the only thing strong enough to overcome hate."

"But I'm afraid of her," I replied, unsure that I could do what he was asking me to do.

"Can you at least feel compassion for her, for all the things that must have happened in her life to make her the way that she is?" he asked. I thought about her being locked up in an attic and being all alone in a hospital room, and I felt truly sorry for her.

"I can do that," I said to the old man, but he had already gotten up from the table and walked away. He always left me with more questions than answers. I finished my homework and put my books into my backpack. I waved goodbye to Miss Peters as I left the library and walked home. My aunt's car was in the driveway. I prepared myself for the tongue lashing that I would get for what happened this morning and for not going directly home after school. I unlocked the door and went inside.

"Lauren, come up here right now!" Aunt Rose yelled from her bedroom. I reluctantly walked upstairs and felt a sense of impending doom with each step I took. I felt like a prisoner walking to their execution. When I finally reached my aunt's bedroom, I could see clothes with their tags still on them strewn all over the bed. Brand new high heeled shoes were still in their box on the dresser.

"There you are," Aunt Rose said as she came out of her walk-in closet dressed in a robe. "You'll never believe what happened. I met with my new client, David Applebottom, today. He's going to be the head chef at a new restaurant in town, and he invited me out to dinner tonight. I had some free time this afternoon, so I went shopping and bought a few things. Let me try on the new dress and you can tell me what you think," Aunt Rose added as she picked up one of the outfits on the bed and went back into the closet to change. I let out the breath that I had been holding. I was so relieved that she wasn't angry with me. A minute later she came out wearing a fitted black dress with intricate beading.

"You look really beautiful, Aunt Rose," I said with sincerity.

"I also bought these shoes to go with it," she said as she took some rhinestone studded high heels out of the shoebox.

"Wow," I said. "They're so sparkly. I love them."

"I do too," Aunt Rose giggled as she sat on the bed and put them on. There was a sudden knock on the front door. "Oh, no. He's here already. Hurry and go downstairs and let him in. I still need to touch up my makeup," she said, panicked. I had never seen Aunt Rose so nervous before.

I went downstairs and opened the door. A tall man with broad shoulders and blue eyes and brown hair stood there.

"Is Rose home?" he asked.

"She'll be down in a minute," I replied before I opened the door wider to let him in. He stepped inside, and his gaze seemed transfixed on something at the top of the stairs. I turned to look, worried that Arabella was standing there, but it was Aunt Rose who was slowly making her way down in her four inch heels. She was gripping the handrail with both hands and trying hard not to fall as her heels wobbled a bit.

"Rose, you look amazing," he said as he reached out his hand to steady her.

"Thank you," she said as a glowing smile spread across her face. "We should get going."

"Goodbye," I said as I watched them leave, but they were too busy staring at each other to hear me. I made sure that the front door was locked although locks never kept out the ghosts. Then I walked over to the kitchen to see what Aunt Rose had left me for dinner. I couldn't find anything. She had forgotten to feed me again. Poopsie came into the room and looked at me expectantly. "I guess we're on our own tonight." I found the last slice of cheese and shared it with the dog. There were still some frozen dinners in the freezer, so I picked one out and put it in the microwave. I found a jar of sweet pickles in the refrigerator and ate them while I waited for my dinner to heat up. The pickles were surprisingly delicious. The frozen dinner wasn't too bad, and I found a half empty jar of strawberry jam that I ate for dessert. After I was finally full, I went upstairs to get ready for bed. I knew the drill. Keep all the lights on and the covers over my head. I reassured myself that I had only had a few nightmares the last couple of nights. They were just bad dreams. They couldn't hurt me. I crawled into bed and closed my eyes. I felt a sickening feeling in the pit of my stomach, and I hoped that it was just the combination of pickles and strawberry jam, but I wasn't sure. I finally fell into a fitful sleep a short time later.

Something sharp dug into my foot, and I opened my eyes. When I looked around I could see that I was no longer in my bedroom. I was standing outside in a field in the middle of nowhere. There was an eerie mist that covered the ground.

"Lauren, come here," a male voice called from a distance. I wasn't sure who it was, and I was worried that it was the old man from the haunted house. Maybe I had done something wrong and he was here to punish me. My heart started to pound rapidly as I looked around for a place to hide, but I could only see flat, barren land around me in the murky darkness. "Lauren, come here," the voice called again. I took an involuntary step toward the voice and then another one. I tried to make myself stop, but I couldn't.

"Wake up," I screamed out loud, but my legs kept moving forward. I pinched myself hard on my arm, but it had no effect. I shivered in my thin pajamas, and I could feel the cold, hard earth beneath my feet. The mist seemed to grow thicker and circle around me as if guiding me to an uncertain destination.

"Lauren, come here." The voice was close now, but I could barely see through the fog.

"It's just a dream. Wake up," I said again, but it was useless as I continued to move forward. Panic seemed to grip me, and my whole body began to shake as I saw a dark figure coming toward me in the distance. "Please, someone help me!" I cried out, but it was too late. The dark figure lunged forward and grabbed my arm. His bony fingers circled around my wrist in a tight grip that sent piercing cold through my body. His eyes locked onto mine, and I was helpless to look away. His face was covered in clown paint, and the garish red lipstick around his mouth made him look like he had a perpetual smile.

"There you are. Someone wants to see you," he said. He pulled out a yellow rose and bowed in front me. His red wig was slightly crooked, and as he bent over, I could see that the back of his head was caved in.

"No," I screamed as tears began to run down my face. I tried hard to pull away, but his grip was too strong. He began pulling me toward a light in the distance. "Please, stop," I begged, but my pleas fell on silent ears.

"Hello, Lauren," said a female voice coming from the light in the distance. It was a kind and loving voice that seemed to soothe some of my fears. The clown released my arm, and I could see Eliza suddenly standing in front of me. It was the ghost that John and I had helped a few months ago. She looked radiant as she stood before me. "You helped me, and now I would like to help you. Find the doll, and you'll find the answers that you're looking for," she said.

"What doll?" I asked, but she had disappeared as quickly as she had appeared. "Wait, come back. What doll?" I asked again. I took a step forward into the darkness and plunged head first into a dark abyss. I screamed as I tried desperately to grab onto to something to stop my fall, but all I could see was endless blackness.

I woke with a start and realized that I was back in my bedroom. My heart was still pounding as I tried to reassure myself that it was just a dream. The sun was just coming up, so I pulled my covers off and got out of my bed. Something soft touched my feet. I looked down, and I could see a few yellow rose petals scattered on the floor. My heart started beating fast again. I remembered that Eliza had told me to find the doll, but I wasn't sure where it was. I had always seen the little girl holding it when she appeared to me. Maybe she had hidden it somewhere in her bedroom. I quickly put on my clothes for school and started searching the room for it. I checked the closet and all the drawers in the dresser, but it wasn't there. I started looking for any hidden compartments in the wall when I suddenly heard a bloodcurdling scream. The sound frightened me, and I jumped. It was coming from Aunt Rose's room. It was followed by the sound of pounding footsteps heading toward my bedroom. I stood there frozen in fear as a large figure appeared in my doorway.

"How could you do this to me?" the voice screamed. I looked up, and I could see Aunt Rose standing there. Her hair was sticking out as if she had been electrocuted, and she had gaudy blue eye shadow around her eyes and bright red lipstick smeared around her mouth.

"It wasn't me, Aunt Rose. I swear."

"Then who did it? The ghost in the house?" she said angrily.

"I think so, but I'm not sure if it was Arabella or the clown." I knew the instant that I had said it that it was the wrong thing to say. I could see the intense fury in my aunt's eyes as she clenched her fist and took a step toward me. A survival mechanism seemed to kick in, and I jumped over my bed and ran past Aunt Rose through the doorway. I raced down the stairs and grabbed my backpack before running out the front door. I was out of breath by the time I reached the school. I looked behind me to see if Aunt Rose had followed me, but no one was there. It was so early that the school was still locked up. I decided to hide behind the school gym, and I found a patch of grass to sit on. A cool breeze caressed my face, and I wrapped my arms around my body to keep warm. My eyelids felt so heavy that I could barely keep them open. The moment I closed my eyes, I fell asleep and for the first time, dreamed of nothing.

Chapter 16

The school bell rang, and it woke me up. I scrambled to get up and ran to my classroom. I saw John just as he was leaving his locker, and I gave him the peace sign to let him know that I needed to talk to him at lunch. Thankfully, Miss Sullivan didn't say anything to me about being late as I sat down at my desk. I tried to concentrate on the history lesson, but my mind started to wander, and I tried to think of where the doll could be hidden. Then I remembered the dream I had about being locked in the attic. When I went to hide from the old man, I crawled into a corner and sat on something. When I pulled it out from under me, I remembered that it was a doll. I was relieved when the bell finally rang for lunch, and I went outside to our secret meeting place and waited for John.

"Is everything OK?" John asked as he sat down beside me. He noticed that I didn't have a lunch and handed me half of his sandwich.

"Thanks," I said as I took a bite out of the peanut butter and jelly sandwich. "Guess who I dreamed about last night?"

"Arabella?" John guessed.

"No. Eliza and the scary clown. Eliza told me that if we find the doll, we'll find the answers that we're looking for."

"What doll?" John asked.

"Arabella's doll. I sometimes see her holding a doll. I searched her bedroom, but it wasn't there. I'm almost positive that it's in the attic. Do you think that you can ask your mom if you can come over after school and help me look?" I begged. I didn't want to go up there alone.

"I guess I could ask her when she comes to pick me up," he offered.

"Thanks, John. Also, one of the ghosts put makeup on Aunt Rose's face while she slept last night, so she's really mad at me," I warned him ahead of time.

"What happened?" John asked, confused.

"One of the ghosts put blue eye shadow and smeared red lipstick all over Aunt Rose's face. I told her that it wasn't me, but she didn't believe me."

"She's not going to be there this afternoon, is she?" John asked. Most people were afraid of Aunt Rose's temper.

"No. She usually doesn't get home before five," I reassured him. The bell rang to go in, and I was grateful that John still wanted to help me. The rest of the afternoon I worked on math problems and took a spelling test. When school finally ended, I waited outside with John until his mom arrived.

"Mom, Lauren wants me to help her with a project. Can I go over to her house?" John asked.

"Sure. Why don't you both get in and I'll drop you off," Mrs. Taylor offered.

"Thank you," I replied gratefully.

"How long do you think it's going to take?" Mrs. Taylor asked.

"You have to pick me up before five," John replied adamantly.

"All right. I'll run a few errands in town and then pick you up," she added as she pulled into my aunt's driveway.

"Thanks, again," I said as I got out of the car. I unlocked the front door, and John and I both left our backpacks in the entryway. The dark, heavy feeling never left the house even with the bright sunlight streaming through the windows.

"Let's go find the doll," I said as I started to climb the stairs before I lost my nerve. John followed behind me. The door to the attic opened more easily this time, but the feeling of fear was just as strong.

"Do you know where it is?" John asked as we stood in the attic.

"I'm pretty sure that it's in that corner," I replied as I pointed to a dark area on the left filled with cobwebs. I wasn't sure what I feared most, spiders, ghosts, or clowns. I took a few steps toward the corner, but John didn't follow me. "Aren't you coming?" I asked, afraid to venture on alone.

"All right," John agreed reluctantly. We stepped over a few boxes and squeezed past an antique dresser.

"I think it was over here," I said as I moved a few boxes to get into the remote corner. I saw a small piece of light blue silk fabric on the floor and I picked it up. As I brushed away the dust, I could see a very ornate porcelain doll with blond curls cascading down under a fancy blue hat. She had a blue silk dress with gold ribbons and small flowers sewn into the dress. She was beautiful. "I found it, John," I exclaimed triumphantly.

"Let me see it," John asked eagerly.

"OK," I said as I handed it to him. I almost made fun of him for being so excited about a doll, but I decided not to. He examined the doll closely.

"Look, someone embroidered something here on the dress. It says, 'For My Flower'. How is that supposed to help us find Arabella's mother?" John asked as he handed the doll back to me.

"I have a special doll that I sent in registered papers for. Maybe there's a serial number on the doll and we can track it back to its original owner," I suggested. I tried to look for a serial number, but I couldn't find one. Suddenly, a dark cloud seemed to have moved across the sky, blocking the few rays of sunlight that had filtered through the window, plunging the room into a depressing gloom. I felt a chill fill in the air, and I could see my breath in front of me. "We should go, John," I said with a sense of urgency.

"OK," John replied, seemingly unaware of the darkness closing in around us. As we were about to reach the door, a strong breeze seemed to rush past us, and the door slammed violently shut in front of us. John jumped a few feet in the air and screamed like a little girl. He ran to the door and tried in vain to open it. The sound of evil laughter filled the attic. Another high pitched scream escaped from John as he grabbed the door handle tighter and jumped up and down as he tried desperately to open the door. Something was moving in one of the dark corners, and the sound of laughter was coming closer.

"Hurry, John. She's coming," I cried.

"I'm trying," John said desperately. I looked toward the corner, and I could see red eyes peering out from the darkness. A glint of silver flashed in her hand, and I could see that she was holding a knife. She seemed to glide over the boxes as she moved toward us. Instead of panic, a strange calm overcame me as I remembered the Native American man telling me to show the spirit love and compassion.

"Arabella," I yelled out loud. "Please, stop. We're trying to help you. We're trying to find your mother," I pleaded. Suddenly, she disappeared and the door opened wide, causing John to lose his balance and fall backwards. Before I could help him up, he propelled himself forward and ran full speed down the stairs while still screaming like a little girl. I tried to follow close behind him, but he was much faster than I was. I ran down the stairs toward the front door, and I wasn't sure if I tripped or I was pushed, but I remember tumbling down the last few stairs and falling flat on my face in the entryway.

"Are you all right?" John asked.

"I think so," I replied, unsure.

"Is she gone?" John asked fearfully. I looked back up at the top of the stairs, but they were empty.

"She's gone," I confirmed.

"Where's the doll?" John asked.

"I dropped it when I fell down the stairs," I replied as I looked around the foyer. I saw the blue silk dress underneath a bench and the doll's head lying a few feet away. "Oh, no. I broke the doll," I cried in distress.

"It's OK, Lauren. I'm sure I can fix it," John replied as he went to pick up the broken pieces. He started to screw the head back on, but there was something sticking out from the doll's body. John looked more closely, and then he pulled out a yellowed piece of paper. "I found something," John exclaimed as he unfolded the piece of paper.

"What is it?" I replied.

"It's a letter," John said.

"What does it say? Hurry and read it," I exclaimed as I could barely contain my excitement.

We were finally going to find out who Arabella's mother was.

"It says, 'Dear Baby Girl, I insisted that your adoptive parents give you the doll that my Grandma Mary had given me when I was a child. When you hold it, I hope that you can imagine that it is me and all the love that I have for you hugging you back. I'm not sure that you will ever find this note, but I needed you to know how much you were wanted and loved. Andrew was so excited when he found out about you, and we had planned to elope that summer, but he was tragically killed in a car accident after graduation. My father forced me to give you up, and my heart shattered into a million pieces the day that the nurses took you from my arms. I will think of you and love you every day until I can finally find you and hold you in my arms once again. Love, Your Mommy.'"

"What's her name? Are you sure that she didn't sign her name somewhere?" I asked. John turned the paper around and looked inside the doll again.

"That's all it says," John replied as he shrugged his shoulders.

"But the dream said that if we find the doll, we'll find the answers," I said, frustrated.

"We know from Sylvia Morgan that the baby's mother lived here in Bozeman. Now we know that she had a grandmother named Mary and that Arabella's birth father's name was Andrew. Maybe we can see if there are any articles online about a high school student killed in a car accident after graduation," John proposed.

"That's a good idea. My aunt left her computer in the dining room," I replied. John and I found the computer and sat down at the table. I placed the doll gently in the box on the floor with the adoption papers.

"Arabella was born in 2000, so I'll type in the name Andrew and the words *car accident* and *graduation* in the year 1999 and 2000 in Bozeman, Montana." There were a few articles that popped up on the screen.

"What about this one?" I asked as I pointed to one of the headlines. John pulled up the article.

"No. This one says that Andrew Brooks was twenty-two years old when he died. He would have had to have flunked several grades to be that old at graduation." John pulled up a few more articles, but either the age was wrong or they were from another town far away. I was starting to feel discouraged.

"Maybe this one," John replied as he started to read it. "No. It says that his wife accidently ran him over and then backed up." There was just one more newspaper article left. I said a silent prayer. John clicked on the link. "This is it," John said. "It says, 'Andrew Campbell, 18, from Bozeman, Montana was killed on June 4, 2000 after driving home from a graduation party. The accident occurred at 10pm on Frontage Road when the driver allegedly swerved to miss a deer and hit a utility pole. The driver of the car was killed instantly, and the passenger was air lifted to a nearby hospital in critical condition. No other cars were involved, and alcohol does not appear to be a factor in the accident.'"

"Does it say who the passenger was? Maybe it was Arabella's mom?"

"No, it doesn't say. I'll try and look for more information," John said as he typed new words into the search engine. After a half hour, John finally looked up from the computer. "I can't find anything more about the passenger, but I did find Andrew Campbell's obituary. It says, 'A funeral service will be held for Andrew Campbell, 18, of Bozeman,

Montana at the Bozeman Cemetery on Saturday, June 10th at 1pm. Andrew was a loving son and is survived by his parents Clyde and Jane Campbell and his aunt, Sylvia Campbell Morgan and her husband, Harold Morgan.'"

"WHAT?" I yelled out loud.

"I know. Can you believe that? Sylvia Morgan was his aunt. She knew all along who Arabella's parents were. We have to go back to the convalescent hospital and make her tell us," John declared.

"Please, John, no. I can't go back. She's crazy, and she called me a murderer. Please, don't make me go back," I begged. "We can find out who his friends were in high school and then ask them. They would know. I'm your friend, and I know that you like Ashley Smith."

"I never told you that," John said defensively.

"You always get this goofy smile every time that you see her. Anyways, that doesn't matter. The point is, if we find his friends, they would know who he was dating."

"How do we find out who his friends were in high school?" John asked.

"I bet they might have pictures of him hanging out with his friends in his high school yearbook. I saw Mom putting away some of the Bozeman High School yearbooks in the library." There was a knock at the door.

"My mom is here. I'll ask her if we can go to the library after school tomorrow," John said as he walked over to pick up his backpack. "And don't tell anyone that I like Ashley, and I won't tell everyone that you're in love with Tommy," John added.

"That's not true. I can't stand Tommy," I said angrily.

"Lauren and Tommy sitting in a tree, K-I-S-S-I-N-G," John sang as he walked out the door and got in the car. I ran after him and stuck my tongue out at him. He just smiled and waved goodbye. He knew how to make me mad. I stomped my foot and then turned around and slammed the front door shut. A moment later, the phone rang, and I went into the kitchen and picked up the phone.

"Hello?" I asked, worried that Arabella might be on the other line.

"Lauren, it's me," Mom replied. She sounded upset.

"Mom, I've missed you so much. Is everything OK?" I asked.

"Rose called me this morning. She said that you put makeup all over her face while she slept last night."

"It wasn't me. I swear." I waited for her to answer, but there was just silence on the other end. "You believe me, don't you?" I cried.

"I believe you," Mom finally replied. "Just try to get along with Rose. I know that she's not the easiest person to be around, but you have a beautiful heart and a kind soul, and I know that you always try to do the right thing."

"Thanks, Mom. I'll try to be nicer to Aunt Rose," I replied, but I couldn't see why Aunt Rose couldn't be nicer to me.

"Anyways, I wanted to tell you that Grandma is doing great, so I booked a flight home. I'll be there on Saturday," Mom announced happily.

"Yaaaay!!!" I screamed. "That's not very long from now," I said as I jumped up and down.

"I know. I can't wait to see you, Pumpkin. I love and miss you so much."

"I love you, too, Mom."

"I'll see you soon," she said before she hung up the phone. I went upstairs to work on my homework. I heard the front door open just as I entered my bedroom, but I wanted to hide from Aunt Rose so I closed my door. An hour later, I heard her calling that dinner was ready. I dragged my feet as I went into the kitchen. Aunt Rose flashed me an angry look. She was still mad at me for what happened this morning.

"I'm sorry I haven't been very nice to you, Aunt Rose. I'll try to be nicer." I refused to specifically apologize for the makeup fiasco since it wasn't me, but I knew that I hadn't always been nice to Aunt Rose, and for that I was truly sorry.

"It's all right, Little Quack Quack. I forgive you," Aunt Rose said as she spooned something unrecognizable onto my plate.

"What is that?" I asked, trying to hide my revulsion.

"It's beef stroganoff," she replied. I said a silent grace, thanking God for bringing my mom home soon, and then I took a bite of what looked like dog food. "How is it?"

"Good," I lied. Poopsie sat expectantly at my feet as I smuggled her pieces of meat when Aunt

Rose wasn't looking. Thank goodness for the dog. "I'm tired. I think I'll go to bed early," I said as I got up to wash my dish and help clear the table. "Is it OK if I go to the library with John after school tomorrow?"

"Sure, as long as you are home by five."

"I will be," I promised. "Goodnight."

"Goodnight, Little Quack Quack."

I walked upstairs to my bedroom and flipped on the light switch. Two black eyes stared at me through the window. I screamed, and the sound startled the raven sitting on the window ledge. "Stop scaring me," I told the bird as I shut the drapes. I put my pajamas on and pulled the covers over my head. I was tired from all the bad dreams, and it didn't take long before I fell asleep.

I woke to the sound of someone walking around my room. I gripped my covers tightly and sunk deeper into my bed. As I listened closely, it almost sounded like someone was playing with the dollhouse in the corner of the bedroom. I decided to pretend that I was asleep in the hope that whoever was there would leave me alone. A short time later, I could hear footsteps leaving my bedroom, followed by the sound of someone falling down the stairs. There was terrible moaning, but I knew it was the old man and that there was nothing that I could do for him. I covered my ears to muffle the sounds. I don't know how much time went by before the haunting organ music began playing and I fell asleep.

I woke up to the sound of my alarm and started getting ready for school. As I bent down to tie my shoe laces, I could see that all the furniture in the dollhouse had been moved around. There was a small male doll. His body was contorted as he laid in a crumpled mass at the bottom of the dollhouse stairs. I felt sick inside as I looked at the disturbing sight and quickly ran out of the room.

Chapter 17

School was incredibly boring today. I ate lunch by myself since I didn't have anything new to tell John and I was meeting him after school to go to the library. When I came in after lunch, Tommy went to sit down at his desk, and then I heard a noise that sounded like a fart. The whole class laughed and made fun of him.

"I didn't fart. It was the desk," Tommy said as his face turned red.

"Sure. The desk farted," another student laughed.

"I believe you, Tommy. I know it was the sound of the desk scooting across the floor," I replied as I turned back around in my seat. It was the truth, and you were supposed to be nice to your enemies.

"Thanks, Lauren," Tommy replied. Miss Sullivan walked in and immediately started the next lesson. School dragged on for another few hours. It was almost time for the bell to ring when I felt something land in my hair. When I pulled it out, I could see that it was a spit wad. I turned around to confront the offending culprit. Tommy sat at his desk with crumpled pieces of paper and a straw.

"How could you do that to me, Tommy, especially when I was nice to you?" I questioned him.

"I know. That's why this time I didn't actually spit on the paper," he replied as he smiled at me. The bell rang, and I quickly gathered up my books before I said or did something that I would regret. Being nice to your enemies was much harder than it looked. I was still furious when I met John outside at the front of the school.

"Trouble with your boyfriend?" John teased when he saw me. I don't know what happened, but I lost it and kicked John in the shins. "Owww!!! What was that for?" John asked.

"You know," I replied angrily as I started to walk towards the library. John ran to catch up with me.

"I'm sorry for teasing you," he apologized.

"I'm sorry I kicked you," I finally replied, and I told him that I was really angry with Tommy for what he had done. John offered to help me, but I didn't know how he could. We finally reached the library, and Miss Gladys Peters greeted us as we walked in.

"Hi, John. Hi, Lauren. What can I help you with today?" Miss Peters asked.

"We wanted to look at some of the yearbooks from Bozeman High School," I replied.

"They're over here in this section," Miss Peters replied as she led us to the back of the library. "Do you know what year you were looking for?"

"The year 2000," I said.

"That's the year that your mom and Rose graduated. I was in the class behind them," Miss Peters commented as she pulled out the yearbook that we were looking for. "Here you go. Let me know if there is anything else that I can help you with."

"Thanks, Miss Peters," I replied as John and I found a table to sit down at. I looked under the senior pictures and found a picture of my mom. She looked so young and pretty. There was no sadness in her eyes or worry lines around her mouth. She looked happy.

"Give me the book. I want to find Andrew Campbell," John said as he pulled the book away from me. John flipped through several pages. "Here he is," John commented as he pointed to a picture. Andrew Campbell looked more like a boy than a man with his tousled blond hair and crooked smile. He had the same piercing blue eyes as Arabella.

"Are there any more pictures of him with his friends or a girlfriend?" I asked.

"Let me check," John said as he went meticulously through the yearbook. "I found another picture of him with some friends," John declared happily. It was a picture of Andrew in a band uniform. Standing next to him was my mom. She was holding a flute, and I remembered her telling me that she was in the band in high school. Next to mom was Aunt Rose holding a tuba, and standing on the other side of Andrew was a young woman with long, blond hair. She had her arm wrapped loosely around Andrew's shoulder, and she was looking up at him and smiling. She looked vaguely familiar.

"Who's that girl?" I asked, pointing to the girl with the long, blond hair.

"There's a caption below this picture. It says her name is Susan Sullivan."

"Susan Sullivan? Could that be my teacher, Miss Sullivan?" I said in disbelief. John and I looked closer.

"Yes. It's her. Do you think that she could be Arabella's mother?" John asked.

"Maybe," I replied. "Are there any more pictures?" John looked through the rest of the yearbook but couldn't find any.

"We should go soon. My mom is going to pick me up at your house."

"OK," I agreed as I put the yearbook away, and we left the library.

"You should ask Miss Sullivan about Arabella when you see her," John told me.

"What am I supposed to say? I don't want to ask her if she had a baby with someone after high school."

"Just ask her if her grandmother's name was Mary. If it wasn't, then we know that it isn't her."

"OK, but we're just a block from the school. Maybe she's still in her classroom and you can come with me and ask her," I begged. This wasn't something that I could do alone.

"I doubt that she's still there, but I guess that we could try."

"Thanks, John," I replied as we went into the school and walked toward my classroom. I peered inside, and I could see Miss Sullivan sitting at her desk correcting papers. She looked up at me.

"Lauren, did you forget one of your books?" she asked.

"No. John and I wanted to ask you something," I replied as I pulled John into the room with me.

"Hi, John. It's so nice to see one of my favorite students from last year."

"Thanks," John beamed.

"What did you want to ask me?"

"We wanted to know what your grandmother's name is," I replied. Miss Sullivan gave me an odd look.

"Her name is Anne," she replied.

"What is your other grandmother's name?" John asked.

"It's Marie," Miss Sullivan said, puzzled.

"Did anyone ever call her Mary?" John replied.

"I think some members of my family might have called her Mary. Why do you want to know?" John and I were silent for a moment. I didn't know what to say next. I finally decided on the truth.

"John and I found some adoption papers in the attic of my aunt's house. We found out that Andrew Campbell was the father of the baby, and we thought that maybe you were…" I couldn't finish the sentence.

"You thought that I was the mother," Miss Sullivan answered. She sat there in silence for the longest time. A tragic look came across her face. "Andrew was my best friend, and I loved him very much. Did you know that I was in the car with him the night of the accident? I tried to help him, but there was nothing that I could do. It was too late. I was airlifted to a hospital nearby with massive internal injuries. I was lucky to be alive, but because of the accident, I can never have children," she said as she wiped a tear from her eye. She tried to compose herself. "I'm glad that Andrew had a baby. He was such a wonderful person." I couldn't tell her that Arabella had died too, so I quickly changed the subject.

"Do you know who Andrew was dating his senior year?" I asked.

"He told me that he had found his true love, but he was very secretive about it. He said that her father was very strict and that she didn't want anyone to find out about them. I remember that he called her his flower," Miss Sullivan added.

"Rose is the name of a flower. Did Andrew ever date Rose?" John piped in.

"I think they went out once or twice in high school, but I don't think they were ever boyfriend and girlfriend." Miss Sullivan paused for a moment. "To be honest, I don't really know. I'm sorry that I can't help you more."

"Thanks for all your help," I replied. "I'm supposed to be home before five, so I better go. Thanks again," I said as I grabbed John's hand and ran out of the room. I was afraid that she'd start asking questions about Arabella and I wouldn't know what to say.

"I can't believe that your Aunt Rose might be Arabella's mother. You have to ask her as soon as you get home," John said, excited. "Maybe that's why she bought the house because she subconsciously knew that her daughter was there."

"I have a tough time believing that Aunt Rose was ever a mother, and she swears that she's never seen or heard anything unusual in the house," I replied. "Besides, I'm afraid to ask her. She's really scary when she gets mad at me."

"I can definitely see where Arabella gets her temper," John replied. He had a point. "Just start out by asking your Aunt Rose what her grandmother's name is."

"What if it isn't Mary?" I asked.

"Then we can still ask your mom. She was friends with Andrew, too. She might know who he was dating," John replied.

"You're right," I said as we walked up to my aunt's house. John's mom was waiting in the driveway.

"I have to go. Don't forget to ask your aunt," John said as he got into the car.

"I won't," I said as I waved goodbye, but I suddenly felt a sinking feeling in the pit of my stomach. My mother's name was Elizabeth Evans, but I remembered that she had an unusual middle name. It was Sunflower. A part of me hoped that

Aunt Rose was Arabella's mother because if she wasn't, there was a strong possibility that Arabella was my sister.

Chapter 18

I walked into the empty house and went into the kitchen to get something to drink. There was a note on the table from Aunt Rose. It said that she was showing David Applebottom a few houses today and then they were going out to dinner. She wanted me to eat the leftover beef stroganoff for dinner. I opened the refrigerator and looked at the dish from last night. There was a thick layer of congealed fat on top. It looked even less appetizing than it did yesterday. Instead, I found a can of soup in the pantry and heated it up on the stove. I put down a bowl of food for Poopsie, and we ate our meager dinner in silence.

I heard a loud knock on the door, and Poopsie started barking. I knew Aunt Rose had a key, so I decided to ignore the knocking and hoped that whoever was there would think that no one was home. Ten minutes later, the knocking still continued. I decided to pull up a chair and look through the peep hole to see who was there. I could see a tall man with dark hair and a mustache standing outside the front door. He was in his thirties and dressed in a formal suit. He seemed to sense that I was looking at him because he stopped knocking.

"Hello. May I please talk to Sara?" he asked.

"I'm sorry. There's no one named Sara here," I replied. He had the wrong house, and I expected him to go away, but a few seconds later the knocking started again. What was wrong with this guy? I was about to pull the chair away and leave the room when he spoke again.

"We've come a very long way. Could you just tell Sara that we're here to see her?" he asked politely. Who else was with him? I got back on the chair and looked through the peephole. Standing beside the man was a young boy about five or six years old. He was wearing knee length pants with stockings and a white ruffled shirt. His clothing looked like it came from the 1800's. The name Sara sounded familiar to me, and it took me a moment to remember that Mrs. Harrison had told me that Sara and Thomas Richards were the original owners of the house on Raventree Lane. Could it be that he was talking about the lady in grey? Could she be the Sara that he wanted to talk to? I didn't know what to do. I had never called a ghost to come to the front door before. The knocking persisted. I finally got up my courage and decided to summon the lady in grey. I hid behind the marble column.

"Sara," I called out with a shaky voice, but no one came. "Sara," I said more loudly this time. The temperature in the foyer began to drop, and I started to shiver. I could hear the sound of footsteps approaching from the dining room. A part of me wanted to run away, but instead I just held on tighter to the marble column as if it could protect me from what was coming. The lady in grey appeared a few feet from me. Her crazed eyes looked directly into mine. My heart began beating wildly, and I could see my breath in front of me.

"Someone is here to see you," I quickly said before I lost my nerve. A panicked look overcame her, and she started to walk over to the organ. I knew that once she started playing, she wouldn't stop until sunrise. She was just about to sit down at the bench when I yelled out, "It's your husband and son." She turned around slowly and looked at me. There was an expression of disbelief on her face. She stood there in silence for the longest time.

"Would you like to see them?" I finally offered. She seemed unsure that I was telling the truth but finally nodded her head yes. I was terrified to leave the column and open the front door. I was afraid of the ghost standing in front of me, and I was afraid of what might be waiting behind the front door. On shaky legs, I took a few tentative steps toward the front door. The lady in grey continued to stand silently by the organ as I unlocked the door. I mustered up what little courage I had left and opened the front door widely as I quickly hid behind it. The lady in grey stood there in shock as she looked out the front door.

"Thomas? Billy? Is that really you?" she asked in astonishment.

"It's me, Mommy. I've missed you," the young boy said gleefully.

"I've missed you, too," Sara replied lovingly as her eyes began to tear up. She continued to stand there in disbelief, afraid that if she took a step forward, the apparitions would disappear.

"My dear Sara, I can't tell you how wonderful it is to see you," Thomas Richards replied warmly as he waited by the front door.

"You've been gone for so long. I was worried that something had happened to you," Sara said fearfully.

"We're here now, my love," Thomas replied as he stretched his hand out toward her. A tear rolled down her face as she took a hesitant step forward.

"Hurry up, Mommy. We've been waiting for you for a long time," Billy said as he jumped up and down with excitement. Sara took another step forward, and the worn threads in her grey dress began to change to a brilliant silver color. Her disheveled white hair was smoothed back into a golden chignon twisted loosely at the back of her neck. With each step she became more youthful and breathtakingly beautiful.

"I love you, my dear Sara," Thomas said as she came closer.

"I love you, too, Mommy," Billy chimed in.

"I love you both so much. More than words could ever say," Sara replied. Tears were streaming down her face as she took the last few steps to the front door and reached out her arms to them. Thomas pulled her close and embraced her tightly. Billy wrapped his arms around her legs and smiled up at her. Sara looked down and gently caressed his soft, curly brown hair. A smile of pure joy lit up her face.

"Thank you," she said as she turned to look at me. Suddenly, there was a bright flash of light, and they were gone. It happened so quickly that I couldn't believe that they had vanished into thin air. I stepped outside the front door and looked down the street, half expecting them to be strolling by. A few fireflies glowed in the dark, and I could hear the sound of crickets chirping, but no one was there. I went back inside and locked the door. I stood there for a moment in awe at what had just happened.

The phone rang suddenly, startling me. It was probably my mom calling. I wasn't ready to ask her any questions about Andrew Campbell and Arabella yet. I went into the kitchen and picked up the phone.

"Hello," I said. There was only static on the other end of the line. "Mom, is that you?" I asked.

"Why are you in my house?" a young voice questioned me. I jumped back in fear as I dropped the phone. I remembered that I was supposed to show compassion, so I hesitantly picked up the phone.

"Arabella, is that you?" I asked. I continued to hear static on the other end. "I'm trying to help you find your mommy."

"Have you found her?" she asked with a hint of hope in her voice.

"I'm not sure, but I'll know very soon," I replied.

"Someone is coming. I have to hide," Arabella whispered, and the phone went dead. I could hear the sound of footsteps upstairs, and I quickly hid under the table. Maybe the old man was back. Whoever it was, I was scared of them too. Poopsie came over to see what was wrong, and I stroked her fur while I waited under the table until the house was silent again. I finally got the nerve to go upstairs and get ready for bed. My bedroom looked the same as it had this morning. I quickly put on my pajamas and crawled into bed with all the lights on. The house was eerily silent for the first time. Maybe Arabella was happy that I was trying to help her and she would leave me alone tonight. It took me a while to fall asleep. I was unused to the quiet. Although I was happy that Sara had found her family and finally moved on, a part of me missed being lulled to sleep by the haunting music that played every night.

Chapter 19

I woke up the next morning and got ready for school. When I went downstairs, I could hear Aunt Rose humming a happy tune as she cooked something on the stove.

"Good morning, Little Quack Quack. I made you breakfast," she said as she placed a plate of pancakes on the kitchen table for me.

"Thank you," I replied, grateful that it wasn't cereal again. I sat down at the table and took a bite. I started to choke as pieces of raw batter and dry flour came spewing out of my mouth.

"Are you OK?" Aunt Rose asked.

"I just swallowed wrong," I replied, trying not to hurt her feelings. I noticed that the edges of the pancakes were crispy and looked like they had been cooked all the way through. I poured syrup on them and took another bite. They were surprisingly delicious. "Thanks, Aunt Rose. It tastes good." I decided that since she was in such a good mood, I'd ask her about Arabella. "What's your grandmother's name?" A part of me was worried that Aunt Rose didn't have a grandmother named Mary and that my mom did.

"On my father's side, my grandmother's name was Victoria, and on my mother's side, it was Mary Rose. I was named after her." A sense of relief washed over me, and I quickly asked my next question.

"Did you know Andrew Campbell?"

"Yes. We dated in high school. He died in a car accident after graduation. Why do you want to know?" she asked. I didn't know how else to ask her, so I just blurted out the question.

"Did you have a baby with Andrew Campbell?" I held my breath as I waited for an answer. Aunt Rose's face began to turn red, and there was a look of fury in her eyes. I began to fear for my life.

"Susan Sullivan told you that, didn't she?" Aunt Rose yelled.

"No. I swear it wasn't Miss Sullivan," I replied.

"She was always jealous of the relationship that I had with Andrew. She's going to ruin everything with David. She can't stand to see me happy. I'm going to go talk to her right now," Aunt Rose said as she angrily grabbed her purse. I was afraid for Miss Sullivan.

"No, Aunt Rose. I swear Miss Sullivan never said anything. Please don't talk to her," I implored. I saw the car keys under some papers on the kitchen countertop and grabbed them while Aunt Rose wasn't looking. I opened the silverware drawer and put the keys inside. "It's getting late. I better go to school," I said as I picked up my backpack and ran out the front door. At least I had bought some time. I ran as fast as I could to warn Miss Sullivan.

When I got to school, I saw John in the hallway and gave him the secret sign that we needed to talk at lunch, and then I went into my classroom. Miss Sullivan showed up a few seconds before the bell rang, so I didn't have time to talk to her. I kept looking outside the window, expecting my aunt to show up. The bell finally rang for lunch, and I went out to meet John.

"So what's wrong?" John asked as he handed me half his turkey sandwich.

"I found out that Aunt Rose has a grandmother named Mary Rose, so I asked her if she had a baby with Andrew Campbell."

"What did she say?" John asked with anticipation.

"She asked me if Miss Sullivan was the one who had told me that and then got really angry. She said that Miss Sullivan was going to ruin everything with David and that she was going to go talk to her. I'm afraid that Aunt Rose is coming to school to beat up Miss Sullivan," I said, distraught.

"That's horrible. If your aunt shows up, come and get me," John replied.

"Are you going to try and stop her?" I asked.

"No. I've never seen a girl fight before," John replied enthusiastically.

"John, that's a terrible thing to say. You know that Miss Sullivan doesn't have a chance against Aunt Rose," I said, upset.

"But you'll still come and get me, won't you?" John asked. I just glared at him. "Well, did she at least admit that she had a baby?"

"Not exactly," I said as I thought about what she had said.

"Then show her the doll, and if she says that it belongs to her, we'll know for sure that your Aunt Rose is Arabella's mother," John concluded.

"That's a good idea," I agreed, but I was too afraid of Aunt Rose right now to ask her any more questions.

"Did you see Arabella again?" John asked as he took another bite out of his sandwich.

"I didn't see her, but the phone rang last night, and it was her on the other end. She wanted to know why I was in her house, and I told her that I was trying to find her mother."

"She called you on the phone?" John asked.

"Yes. She's called me before. It's really scary," I replied.

"Did you see the number that she was calling from?"

"No. It's a home phone, not a cell phone," I replied.

"You can still find out where the call is coming from. You can either press *69, or if that doesn't work, some phones actually store the last few numbers," John said.

"I didn't know that," I replied. "Can you come over and show me how to find the numbers on the phone?" I didn't want to be alone in the house.

"My mom is dropping me off at the library after school. I have to read a biography and write a paper on it. Maybe you can come with me and then we'll walk to your house afterwards," John suggested.

"OK. I'll see you after school," I replied, grateful that he wanted to help me. The bell rang, and we went back inside. I still stared out the window of my classroom, worried that Aunt Rose would show up, but she never did. When school finally ended, I found John waiting at the front of the school for me.

"My mom said that she would drive us both to the library and then she would pick me up at your house at five o'clock.

"That sounds great," I said as we walked over to his mom's car and got inside. "Thanks, Mrs. Taylor."

"You're welcome," she replied. "How are your mom and grandmother?"

"Fine. Mom is coming home on Saturday," I replied happily.

"That's wonderful news," she said. Not long after, she pulled into the library parking lot. "I'll see you both later." John and I got out of the car and went into the library. Miss Peters was sitting at the front desk.

"Hi, John. Hi, Lauren. Did you ask your aunt if I could take you out to dinner tomorrow night?" she asked.

"I'm sorry. I forgot, but I'll ask her as soon as I get home," I replied apologetically.

"As long as she says yes, why don't you meet me here after school and we can go out to dinner as soon as I get off work," Miss Peters said warmly.

"OK. I'll see you tomorrow," I waved as I turned to follow John upstairs. I found a desk to sit at and started doing my homework while John looked for a book. I was busy working on math when I looked up and found the old Native American man sitting across from me.

"How is it going with the spirit that haunts you?" he asked.

"I think I may have found her mother, but I'm not sure yet," I replied, hopeful.

"Is she more at peace?" he asked.

"Not really. I think that she's still very angry at her adoptive father. She rearranged all the furniture in the dollhouse and put a broken male doll at the bottom of the dollhouse staircase."

"Then your spirit is a poltergeist," the Native American man commented.

"What's that?" I asked.

"A poltergeist is a troubled spirit that has the ability to move things. They often have tremendous energy and can cause electrical interference. Sometimes it can be a young person that is unaware of what they are doing," he said.

"It's not me," I replied defensively.

"I know, but your fear can feed the poltergeist, making it even stronger than it was before. You must not have any fear or you will make things worse," he warned. The thought terrified me.

"But it's really hard not to be afraid. Arabella's scary," I whined, but he never heard me. He had already gotten up from the table and walked away.

"Are you ready to go?" John asked. I jumped. He had startled me.

"Sure," I said as I packed up my homework. We went downstairs, and John checked out his book with Miss Peters. "I'm looking forward to dinner, Miss Peters," I said as she helped John. I truly was looking forward to a decent meal.

"I am too. I'll see you tomorrow, Lauren," Miss Peters smiled. John and I walked out of the library and headed toward my aunt's house. Dark clouds had filled the sky, and a cold wind whipped my hair into my face. I pulled my hair back and buttoned up my coat.

"What book did you get?" I asked.

"I found a biography on Theodore Roosevelt. He was the 26th President of the United States. Did you know that he owned a cattle ranch in North Dakota?"

"I didn't know that," I replied.

"He was a real cowboy," John said admiringly.

"That's great," I said. "Did you see the old Native American man in the library?"

"No. I didn't see him," John replied.

"He told me that Arabella was a poltergeist."

"What's a poltergeist?" John asked.

"It's kind of an angry spirit with a lot of energy that can move things. They can also affect electrical stuff," I explained.

"That's why she can use the phone. I can't wait to find out where the call is coming from. I bet it's coming from inside the house," John replied excitedly.

"That's scary. The old man told me not to be afraid or I would make the spirit even stronger," I told John.

"OK, but it's still pretty cool that she can call on a phone," John added. I didn't think that it was cool, but I was grateful that John wanted to help me. As we neared the house, I could see my aunt's car in the driveway. I was afraid to go inside. When I opened the front door, Aunt Rose was standing in the foyer.

"Have you seen my car keys?" she asked, furious.

"No," I lied as I crossed my fingers behind my back.

"I can't find them anywhere. David had to come and pick me up so that I could show him a house that he wanted to see. I got you dinner at a fast food restaurant on our way home," she said as she shoved a white paper bag into my hands. "David will be here any minute to pick me up for dinner," Aunt Rose said as she glanced out the window.

"Ask her about the doll," John said as he nudged me.

"Ask me about what?" Aunt Rose questioned.

"I was wondering if I could go out to dinner with Miss Peters tomorrow?" I asked.

"Sure, that's fine," she replied as she glanced out the window again.

"You're chicken," John said to me.

"What's this about chicken?" Aunt Rose asked.

"John wanted to know if you got me chicken for dinner," I improvised.

"No. It's a hamburger and fries," she replied. There was a knock at the door. "David's here," Aunt Rose said nervously as she tried to smooth her frizzy hair. "Be good, Little Quack Quack." John snickered as Aunt Rose went out the front door.

"Let's go check out the phone," I said hastily before John started asking more questions about my nickname. I went into the kitchen and put the bag on the table.

"Can I have some french fries?" he asked.

"OK," I said as I found a plate and dumped the hamburger and fries out on it. John started eating all the fries, and it took every ounce of will power not to slap his hand away. I was starving, but he had always shared his lunch with me, so I should do the same. I went to get a knife to cut the hamburger in half, and that's when I saw the car keys in the silverware drawer. I went and placed them on the table by the front door for Aunt Rose to find and hoped that I didn't get in trouble. When I went back to the kitchen, I cut the hamburger down the middle. "You can have half," I told John.

"Thanks, Lauren," John said with a mouth full of french fries. All the food was gone within a few minutes. "Where's the phone?" John asked.

"Right here," I said as I got up and retrieved it from the kitchen counter and gave it to him.

"I'll try *69 first," he said.

"This feature is not available," an automated voice replied on the other line.

"I'll see if I can find the last few calls. They still might be stored on the phone," John said as he started pushing buttons. Fifteen minutes later John finally declared, "I found the numbers. The first number is a 949 area code."

"That's my grandma's area code. My mom must have called today while I was gone," I said, disappointed that I had missed her call.

"This next number came in last night around eight o'clock," John replied.

"That's around the time that Arabella called me," I confirmed.

"I'll write it down and then we can call it and see who answers the phone," John said as he scribbled the number onto the paper bag on the table. Suddenly, there was a strong gust of wind, and the front door blew open. An eerie sound reverberated through the house. John got up to close the door. "It probably wasn't shut all the way," he said when he got back, but I could tell that he was scared too.

"Could you call the number?" I asked.

"Why don't we both dial it together and put it on speaker?" he suggested.

"OK," I agreed as I punched in the first few numbers and he put in the last ones. The phone rang a few times before someone picked it up.

"Granite Springs Hospital. How can I help you?" a woman's voice asked. Neither John nor I knew what to say. "Hello. Is anyone there?" she asked. A few seconds later she hung up.

"What do we do next?" I asked John.

"I guess we can look up the hospital on the internet and find out more about it," John replied.

"I'll go get my aunt's laptop," I said as I went into the dining room and retrieved it. John immediately typed in some words and pulled up a website.

"Here it is," John said as he pointed to a picture. It was a tall, gothic building with a crumbling stone exterior. It looked more like a prison with bars on the windows and depressing grey paint.

"That's exactly like the hospital that I saw in my dream," I exclaimed.

"It must have been the hospital that Sylvia Morgan took Arabella to. It says that it's a mental institution located in Billings, Montana. I guess that Arabella was mentally ill," John surmised.

"I wonder what happened to her," I replied sadly, knowing that it must have been horrible staying there.

"Maybe one of the other patients killed her and now she wanders the halls, calling home," John guessed.

"You're scaring me, John. Maybe she just got really sick and died," I replied.

"Why don't we call the hospital back and see if anyone remembers Arabella," John suggested.

"I don't think they're allowed to talk about any patients," I replied.

"All we can do is try," John said. The wind seemed to have picked up, and the lights flickered.

"OK. We can try." I picked up the phone and tried to dial the number, but there was only silence on the other end. "I think that there's something wrong with the phone," I said. John took the phone out of my hands and tried the number.

"The phone is dead. It must be the storm. We can try again tomorrow," John suggested.

"What if no one remembers Arabella?" I asked.

"We can always go back and talk to Sylvia Morgan. She's probably the only person who really knows what happened to Arabella," John replied. The thought of going to see the old witch again horrified me, but a part of me needed to know what happened to Arabella. Even if we found her birth mother and she was able to move on, I still wanted to know her whole story and how it ended.

"OK. We can go see Sylvia Morgan," I reluctantly agreed.

"I'll ask my mom if we can go to the convalescent hospital after school tomorrow," John said.

"All right," I replied timidly because I was still scared to death of the old hag. There was a loud knock at the door, and it startled me.

"It's probably my mom," John said as he picked up his backpack. I walked with him to the front door. "Don't forget to ask your aunt about the doll," John reminded me.

"I won't," I said dismally. When John opened the door, a cold gust of wind assaulted us.

"Hi, Lauren," John's mom replied when she saw me standing there.

"Hi, Mrs. Taylor," I said.

"There's supposed to be a bad storm tonight. Don't forget to close all the windows," she recommended.

"I'll go do that right now. I'll see you tomorrow, John."

"Bye," he said as he walked out the front door and I watched them leave. I was sad to see them go, and the thought of being alone in the house alarmed me. I locked the front door and then walked through the whole house making sure that all the windows were closed. I thought I saw a dark shadow run across the front yard, but when I looked again, no one was there. I blamed it on the fact that I was especially jumpy tonight because of the storm. My only consolation was that Arabella couldn't call me since the phone was dead. I gave Poopsie a snack before I went upstairs and got ready for bed. It was the same routine. Keep all the lights on and sleep with a flashlight. I remember hearing the faint sounds of thunder in the distance before I finally fell asleep.

A loud clap of thunder woke me, and it took me a moment to realize where I was. The electricity must have gone off because of the storm, and my bedroom had been plunged into complete darkness. I tried the flashlight, but it wouldn't turn on. I thought I heard the sound of the front door opening, but I wasn't sure. Not long after, I could hear the sound of footsteps coming up the stairs. Aunt Rose must be home. I pulled the covers over my head and pretended to be asleep. I didn't know if she was still mad at me. I heard the creaking of my door as it was slowly opened. I could sense someone standing there in the doorway. I slowed my breathing so that my aunt would think that I was asleep and would go away. Instead I could hear the sound of footsteps coming closer to my bed. The room became cold, and I felt a dark presence looming over me. I gripped my covers tighter as I started to shiver. I listened closely for any more movement, but all I could hear was the sound of water dripping onto the floor.

"Aunt Rose, is that you?" I finally asked. Suddenly, my covers were ripped off of my bed. I tried to grab them, but it was too late. There was a flash of lightning, and I could see Arabella standing over me. Her matted hair was plastered to her head, and her gown was soaked through as if she had been out in the storm. Her crazed eyes looked directly at me. I tried to move away from her, but she quickly grabbed my wrist. Her ice cold fingers sent waves of sheer terror through my body.

"Have you found my mommy?" she asked as she continued to stare at me intensely with her demented gaze. I remembered that the Native

American man had told me not to be afraid or it would make her stronger, but I couldn't stop the feelings of intense fear that overwhelmed me.

"I think I found her, but I'm not sure. I'll know soon," I finally answered with a shaky voice. I hoped that my answer would appease her and that she would go away, but she continued to grip my wrist tightly. I heard the sound of heavy footsteps coming down the hallway, and a dark shadow filled the doorway to my room.

"Lauren, who are you talking to?" Aunt Rose asked. She reached inside the bedroom and tried to turn on the light, not realizing that the electricity was off. There was another flash of lightning, and Aunt Rose let out a bloodcurdling scream. "Who are you? What are you doing in my house? Get out or I'm calling the police," she yelled. Arabella released the grip on my arm and took a few steps back in fear. She seemed startled. I looked at Aunt Rose, and I could see that she was staring directly at Arabella.

"You can see her?" I asked my aunt in disbelief. Aunt Rose never answered me. Instead, she lunged forward and pulled me out of my bed. She half dragged me down the stairs. I looked back expecting a ghostly figure to be following us, but no one was there. Aunt Rose seized her purse and keys on the table in the entry way and flung the front door open. We ran out in the pouring rain to the car.

"Get in the car and lock the doors," Aunt Rose shouted. Once we were inside, she pulled out her cell phone and called 911.

"911, what's your emergency?" a voice on the other end replied.

"There's someone in my house," my aunt said frantically.

"It's a poltergeist, Aunt Rose," I replied, but she never heard me. She was busy giving the address of the house to the 911 operator.

"Yes, I'll stay on the line until the police come," Aunt Rose said. I felt somewhat vindicated that my aunt had finally seen Arabella. Now she could no longer claim that the house wasn't haunted. We sat there in silence while we waited. The sound of the rain pounding on the car was deafening. I looked at the house as it towered ominously over us. I waited for the ghostly figure to come walking out the front door, but the house remained dark.

"What's taking the police so long to get here? They better not be out eating donuts," she said, incensed.

"That's not very nice, Aunt Rose," I admonished. There was a loud knock on the car window, and we both jumped.

"Are you the one who called about an intruder in your house?" the police officer asked.

"Yes. That was me," Aunt Rose confirmed.

"Please wait here in the car while my partner and I check it out," the police officer instructed.

"OK," she said. "The police are here," Aunt Rose said to the 911 operator before she put the phone down.

We watched the two police officers enter the haunted house with their flashlights. I could tell that they were in the parlor as their lights shined through the window. They passed through the dining room and kitchen before the house was dark again. A few minutes later I could see a bright light in my bedroom casting an eerie glow throughout the room. The light soon appeared again in Aunt Rose's bedroom before the house was pitch-black again. Time seemed to go by slowly as I waited for the police officers to come back outside. Suddenly, a ghostly apparition appeared in the attic window. A light from behind illuminated the terrifying figure. Her skin was an unearthly pale color and her wild eyes looked desperately out the window at me. She let out an ear piercing howl that sounded more like an animal than a human being. I put my hands over my ears and closed my eyes, afraid of what I had just seen. When I finally opened my eyes, the house was dark again.

"What happened?" I asked.

"I don't know. I can't see a thing without my glasses," Aunt Rose replied as she squinted her eyes to try and see better. A few minutes later the first police officer came out the front door and started walking toward the car. The second police officer followed behind him holding someone in handcuffs. I scooted closer to the window to get a better look. The figure in handcuffs suddenly broke free and started running straight to the car.

"Lock the doors," Aunt Rose screamed. "Hurry, lock the doors," she said frantically as she started pushing all the buttons in the car. The police officer tackled the person a few feet from my window. She was a young girl wearing a hospital gown. I peered out, and I could see Arabella's blue eyes staring back at me.

"No. It's not possible. She's alive," I said in shock. Arabella was small for her age, and her skin was a deathly pale color, as if it had never seen the sun.

"I just want my mommy. Please, find my mommy," she cried pitifully as she struggled to get away from the police officer. She sounded more like a lost child than a criminal, and my heart bled for her.

"I'll find your mommy for you, I promise," I said to her as I pressed my face up against the window. I wasn't sure if she could hear me, but she seemed to calm down, and the officer picked her up and put her in the back of the police car. There was a knock on the window.

"It's safe to go back inside," the other police officer said.

"Thank you," Aunt Rose replied, but neither of us moved. We watched the police officers drive away as we sat there in stunned silenced. The storm was finally starting to pass, and I could see the lights suddenly turn on in my bedroom as the electricity was restored. "Let's make a run for it," Aunt Rose blurted out as she unlocked the car door and ran full speed toward the house, leaving me behind. I ran as fast as I could behind her, and she locked the front door once we were both safely inside. Aunt Rose went over to the liquor cabinet and poured herself a drink. I stood there shivering in my damp pajamas.

"Can I sleep with you tonight?" I asked, afraid that she would say no.

"Of course. I was just about to suggest it myself," she said as she took a big gulp of her drink. I waited for her to go upstairs and followed closely behind her. "You need to change out of your wet pajamas before you catch a cold."

"OK," I said reluctantly because I was afraid to go back into my bedroom. Luckily, I found a dirty pair of pajamas on the bathroom floor and changed into them. I wanted to tell Aunt Rose all about Arabella, but when I went back into her bedroom, she was snoring. I crawled into bed next to her and pulled what little covers were left around myself. I still couldn't believe that Arabella was alive. I laid there for hours in shock before I finally fell asleep.

Chapter 20

When I woke up, Aunt Rose was already downstairs. I was determined to ask her about the doll. I had promised Arabella that I was going to find her mother, and that's exactly what I was going to do. I hurried to get dressed and then went downstairs to the dining room where I had left the doll in the box with all the adoption papers. I noticed that there were tiny roses sewn into the dress. It must be Aunt Rose's doll. A part of me felt sorry for Arabella that Aunt Rose was her mother, but maybe they could make each other better. I held the doll in my arms as I walked into the kitchen. I was surprised to find that Aunt Rose was not alone. David Applebottom was sitting at the kitchen table holding her hand while another man sat across from them holding a clip board.

"Good morning, Little Quack Quack. You remember David, don't you?" she asked. I nodded yes. "And this is Bill. He's here to give me an estimate on installing a security system in the house." She looked at the doll that I was holding in my arms, and a look of shock came across her face. "Where did you find that doll?" she asked, surprised.

"I found it in the attic. Is it your doll?" I replied, hopeful that she would admit that the doll belonged to her.

"No, it's not mine," she said as she purposely she looked away from me. I walked closer to her and held the doll in front of her face.

"Are you sure? Look again," I pleaded. This was not going the way that I had planned.

"I'm positive that it's not mine. I was never into frilly dolls like your mother was," she said firmly. No, it wasn't possible that the doll belonged to my mom. My mom's grandmother on her mother's side was named Deborah, but I couldn't remember the name of her other grandmother. She was from Italy and had died before I was born. I prayed that her name wasn't Mary.

"Did you ever meet my mom's grandmother from Italy?" I asked Aunt Rose.

"Yes, I met her at your mom's wedding. Why do you ask?"

"I was just wondering if you remembered her name," I replied.

"Actually, I do. I remember that she had the same name as my grandmother. It was Mary," she said. In that moment my whole world collapsed. "Lauren, you look pale. Is everything all right?" she asked, concerned. I stood there in shock. "Well, it's all been too much with the break in. Why don't you sit down and I'll get you breakfast. David made the most delicious omelet," she said as she came back with a plate for me. It was a beautiful omelet with vibrant colors and a sauce drizzled elegantly around the plate.

"Thank you," I said as I took a bite. It could have been the best omelet in the world, but I could barely taste anything since my heart had sunk into my stomach. "I should probably go to school," I said glumly as I finished the last bite on my plate.

"I was supposed to do an open house this afternoon, but I'll cancel it so that I can be here when you come home from school," Aunt Rose offered.

"No. Remember I told you that I'm having dinner with Miss Peters tonight. I'm supposed to meet her at the library after school. Please, I really want to go," I begged, afraid that I would get cheated out of a decent meal. I also wanted to spend the least amount of time possible in the spooky house.

"All right. You can go. I should be home before you get back," she replied. "Don't forget your lunch. David made it for you."

"Thanks. I'll see you later," I said as I picked up my lunch with the doll still tucked under my arm. "Thanks, Mr. Applebottom, for the omelet and for lunch."

"You're welcome," he said as he smiled. I went into the dining room and placed the doll back in the box with the adoption papers. I was devastated that Aunt Rose said that it didn't belong to her. I walked out the front door, confused over what I had just learned. I couldn't believe that my mom might be Arabella's mother. It wasn't possible. The doll had to belong to Aunt Rose. It seemed like she had recognized the doll when she first saw it. Maybe she didn't want to admit anything in front of Mr. Applebottom. That must be the reason why she said it wasn't hers. I should ask her again about the doll and tell her all about Arabella this evening when no one was there. It was a good plan, and I felt more hopeful by the time I arrived at school. I saw John and gave him the signal to meet me for lunch in our secret place. I had so much to tell him. When I went into my classroom, I was swarmed by my classmates.

"I heard that someone broke into your house and tried to murder you in your bed," Tommy said dramatically.

"My dad told me that it was a person who had escaped from a mental hospital," another boy added. I didn't know what to say. Miss Sullivan suddenly appeared.

"Everyone please go sit back down at your desks. Lauren has been through a lot, and I'm sure that the police are handling the matter. Please take out your science book and start reading chapter three," Miss Sullivan instructed. I was relieved that I didn't have to answer any questions. It was hard concentrating on school after everything that had happened, and I was happy when the bell finally rang for lunch. I went out to the bench behind the school gym and waited for John. Mr. Applebottom had made my lunch, and I was pleasantly surprised to find a tasty looking sandwich and some snacks inside.

"I heard that someone broke into your aunt's house last night. Are you OK?" John asked, with concern as he sat beside me.

"It was Arabella," I replied with a mouthful of egg salad sandwich.

"What? No, that's not possible. Arabella is a ghost, and I thought that the police arrested someone," John replied, confused.

"Arabella isn't a ghost. She's alive, and she was in the house last night," I said.

"But I don't understand how she could be haunting the house and still be alive?" John questioned.

"I don't really understand it either, but the Native American man told me that poltergeists can sometimes be real people that have no idea that they're doing it. Arabella was locked up in a hospital, and maybe she focused all her energy on the only home that she had ever known," I replied.

"Or maybe she broke out of the hospital weeks ago and has been living in the attic," John guessed. The thought terrified me.

"It's possible," I said. I didn't want to tell John that I had trouble telling the living from the dead and that there was a strong possibility that he was right. Then all the times that I saw her, she was really there. Fear started to overwhelm me.

"Did you tell your aunt about Arabella?" John asked. His question seemed to stop the terrifying train of thoughts that I was having.

"No. Aunt Rose fell asleep before I could tell her anything, but I did ask her about the doll. She said it wasn't hers, but Mr. Applebottom was there, and I think that she didn't want to say anything in front of him. I'm going to ask her again tonight," I replied.

"OK, but if she says it isn't hers, you can always ask your mom. She might know," John added.

"Mom's coming home tomorrow. I can ask her then," I replied. I wasn't ready to tell John that Mom had a grandmother named Mary or that she liked fancy dolls. Sometimes not knowing the truth was easier. The bell rang to go in.

"Tell me as soon as you find out anything," John said as we walked back to our classrooms.

"I will," I promised. I just prayed that it was the answers that I wanted to hear. The afternoon classes went by quickly, and I was glad when school finally ended. I walked over to the library, excited to have dinner with Miss Peters. I found her upstairs helping someone on a computer.

"Hi, Lauren. I should be done in an hour. Why don't you find a place to sit and I'll find you when I'm ready?" Miss Gladys Peters whispered.

"OK," I replied. I walked around the entire library looking for the Native American man. He had some explaining to do, but he was nowhere to be found. I found a book on ghosts and sat down to read it. A few pages into the book, I realized that whoever had written it clearly had never met any ghosts.

"Are you ready to go?" Miss Peters asked. I quickly hid the book that I was reading.

"Yes," I said as I picked up my backpack. "Where are we going?"

"I was thinking about Chinese food. My cat, Chow Mein, just loves it and so do I," Miss Peters said enthusiastically.

"Sounds good to me," I said. I would have been happy with anything. Miss Peters walked me to her car and drove to a small restaurant nearby. The lady at the front showed us to a table and took our order.

"So how are things going with your aunt?" Miss Peters asked.

"You didn't hear. Someone was in the house last night, and the police came and arrested them," I replied.

"Oh, dear. Are you OK? They didn't hurt you?" Miss Peters asked, upset.

"No. I'm fine," I replied.

"You should come and stay with me," she insisted.

"Thanks, but Mom is flying in tomorrow and taking me home. I've really missed her, and I can't wait to go home."

"I'm so glad to hear that. I've missed her too," Miss Peters added. The food arrived, and it looked delicious. I barely said a word as I tried to use the chopsticks to shovel the food into my mouth. Miss Peters talked more about her cats. She mentioned that Cheese Fondue and Peanut Butter weren't getting along. I thought that was a bad food combination as well. By the end of dinner, I felt more at peace. Miss Peters always had a way of making me feel better.

"I guess I should take you back to your aunt's house," she said after we had finished.

"Thanks for dinner," I replied.

"You're welcome," she smiled. It was a short drive to my aunt's house, and I could see that Aunt Rose's car wasn't in the driveway.

"I don't think that my aunt's home yet. Could you stay with me until she gets home?" I asked. I was afraid to be in the house alone.

"Of course. I've always wanted to see inside this house," Miss Peters replied. We walked up the driveway, and I opened the front door. "Oh, this is such a grand entry," Miss Peters commented. I glanced up toward the stairs, half expecting Arabella to be there, but no one was there.

"I can give you a tour. This is the parlor, which I think is a fancy word for living room," I said as I led her through the house. "This is the dining room."

"The chandelier and dining room table are exquisite," Miss Peters said in awe as she walked around the dining room. She suddenly tripped and fell down.

"Are you OK?" I asked.

"Clumsy me. I must have tripped over this box," she replied as she got up. "What a beautiful doll," she commented as she picked it up and ran her hands over the doll's silk dress. Then she put her hand around the doll's head and ripped it off.

"Ahhhhhhh," I screamed as I looked at the decapitated doll.

"Lauren, I'm so sorry. I don't know what overcame me. Don't worry. The head screws right back on," she said as she desperately tried to put the doll back together. I reached down into the box of papers and pulled out the yellowed note that had been tucked inside the doll.

"Were you looking for this?" I asked as I handed her the letter. Miss Peters face turned white. She looked visibly shaken as she collapsed into one of the dining room chairs.

"You know then," she confirmed as she sat there in silence.

"But I thought that the doll belonged to someone named Flower?" I replied, unable to comprehend that the doll belonged to Miss Peters.

"My name is really Gladiolus. I was named after the flower, but most people call me Gladys for short. My Grandma Mary and Andrew were the only ones who called me by my real name," she explained. She began to read the yellowed letter, and tears began streaming down her face. "I loved Andrew so much. We were going to get married as soon as I turned eighteen that summer. When he died, I just couldn't go on. My father forced me to give up my baby. He said that an older wealthy couple that lived here in Bozeman wanted to adopt her. I knew the moment that the nurse took her from my arms that I had made a huge mistake. I loved her and I wanted to keep her, but it was too late. I stayed here in Bozeman and got a job at the library to be near her. I wondered every time a little blond girl came into the library if she was mine," Miss Peters sobbed as she held the doll. "She was such a beautiful baby, so perfect. Not a single day has gone by since she was born that I haven't thought about her." I could hear the pain and anguish in her voice, and it broke my heart. Both of them had suffered greatly. Miss Peters wiped the tears from her face and looked down at the doll. "Where did you find the doll?" she asked.

"John and I found it in the attic," I replied.

"Did my little girl live here?" she asked.

"I think so. There was an older couple that owned the house before my aunt."

"Do you know what happened to my baby?" Miss Peters whispered as if she was afraid to hear the answer.

"I'll be right back," I said as I ran into the kitchen to find the paper bag that John had written the phone number to the hospital on. It was still on the countertop by the phone. I brought it back to Miss Peters. "Your daughter's name is Arabella Morgan, and she's staying at a hospital. This is the phone number," I replied as I handed her the paper bag.

"Is she sick?" Miss Peters asked worriedly.

"I don't really know what's wrong with her," I replied honestly. I couldn't tell Miss Peters that her daughter was in a mental institution. She would find out soon enough. "Arabella knows about you."

"She does?" Miss Peters said, surprised.

"Yes. She's wanted to meet you for a very long time," I replied. The sound of the front door opening interrupted our conversation.

"Please, don't tell anyone about this," Miss Peters begged.

"Can I tell John? He helped me find the adoption papers and the doll," I replied.

"All right, but only John," she said as she brushed away her tears and tried to compose herself before Aunt Rose walked into the dining room.

"Hi, Gladys. Hi, Little Quack Quack. Did you two have a nice dinner?" she asked.

"It was delicious," I replied. Miss Peters could barely say anything.

"I should probably be going," Miss Peters said as she stuffed the paper bag with the phone number into her purse and headed toward the front door.

"Thank you for taking Lauren out to dinner," Aunt Rose replied. I picked up the doll and ran out the front door to Miss Peters.

"You forgot this," I said as I handed her the doll. She looked at me standing there and wrapped her arms tightly around me and held me for the longest time.

"Thank you, Lauren. Thank you so much," she kept saying as tears streamed down her face, only this time, they were tears of joy. She reluctantly let me go and said goodbye. I went back inside and went upstairs and started to get ready for bed. I was just climbing into bed when Aunt Rose popped her head into my room.

"Goodnight, Little Quack Quack. Are you OK?" she asked, concerned.

"I'm fine," I replied. I felt happy that I had finally found Arabella's mother.

"I'm sorry about last night. I don't think that your mother is ever going to let you stay with me again," Aunt Rose said remorsefully.

"It's OK. It wasn't your fault," I said, trying to make her feel better, but deep down inside I was ecstatic that I would never have to come back here.

"Sweet dreams," she said as she smiled.

"Goodnight," I replied. I kept the bedside lamp on and pulled the covers over my head. One can never be too sure about ghosts. I hadn't slept very much the night before, so it didn't take long before I fell asleep.

I woke to the sound of the rocking chair creaking as it rocked back and forth. I pulled the covers tighter around myself as I started to shiver in my bed. Someone was in the room with me. I could sense that they were watching me. Maybe Arabella or her poltergeist had come back. She probably didn't know yet that I had found her mother. The sound of the creaking of the chair was incessant, and I finally got up the courage to say something.

"Arabella, your mother is Gladys Peters, and she's coming to see you soon," I whispered, hoping to appease her. The rocking stopped suddenly. I held my breath as I listened for any more sounds. It was silent for a long time, and I started to relax. Suddenly, I could hear footsteps as someone walked over to my bed. I tried to scoot away, but a heavy weight landed on my legs, trapping me where I was. I wanted to scream, but nothing came out. It felt like ice running through my legs up my body, virtually paralyzing me in my bed. I laid there in fear, unable to move or speak. I could finally hear a male voice speaking to me.

"I'm sorry that I scared you," the voice said. With shaking hands, I pulled my covers down from my face to see who was talking to me. The old man that I had seen die at the bottom of the stairs was staring back at me. It was Harold Morgan.

"It's OK. I forgive you," I said as my voice quivered. A worried look crossed his face.

"Do you think that Arabella will forgive me for what I've done to her?" he asked. I thought about the crazed girl that the police had arrested the other night. She was so full of anger and hate, and I didn't think that she would be forgiving him anytime soon. He stood there staring at me with his brow furrowed, waiting for an answer. I didn't know what to say. The truth was too hurtful. I decided to tell him what I had learned at church.

"Pastor Joe said that if you are truly sorry for what you've done and ask for forgiveness, God will forgive all your sins, no matter what they are," I whispered.

"Do you really think so?" he asked, uncertain.

"I know so," I replied without a doubt. The worried look on his face disappeared, and he seemed more at peace. He reached his hand toward me and touched my hand. I braced myself for his icy touch, but all I felt was warmth.

"Thank you," he said as a smile spread across his face, and he got up and walked away. I laid there in bed, hopeful that the old man could finally move on now.

The house was silent for a while, and I was just about to fall asleep when I suddenly heard the sound of footsteps coming up the stairs again. I didn't know if the old man had more questions for me or if someone else was there. I couldn't handle all the ghosts anymore, so I pulled my covers off and hid under the bed. The sound of footsteps was louder now, and I could hear a clicking noise as someone walked over the hardwood floor toward my bed. A bead of sweat rolled down my forehead, and I held my breath so that I wouldn't make a sound and give away my hiding place. The edge of the bed skirt began to lift up, and two black eyes stared back at me. I was just about to scream when I realized that it was Poopsie.

"You scared me," I said as I let out a sigh of relief. She tried to lick my face as I started to crawl out from under the bed. "You've never been upstairs before," I commented as I stroked her fur. "Let me get you a blanket, and you can sleep in my room," I said, grateful for her company. I found an old quilt in the closet and put it on the floor for her. Poopsie curled up into a ball on top of the quilt and closed her eyes. I got back into bed, but after all the excitement, it was hard to sleep. I was hopeful that all the ghosts had moved on. My eyes finally got so heavy that I couldn't keep them open, and for the first time, I dreamed of angels.

Chapter 21

The next morning I woke up excited that Mom was finally coming home. I put all my clothes into my suitcase and brought it downstairs. I was so happy that I didn't even mind that Aunt Rose served me the disgusting birdseed cereal for breakfast again. Mom's flight was arriving that afternoon, and Aunt Rose and I went to the airport to pick her up. I could hardly wait to see her, and I hopped from one foot to another as I looked for her among all the passengers that were coming off the plane. I finally saw her and waved as I jumped up and down. She looked tired. There were fine lines around her mouth, and she looked worried.

"There you are, Pumpkin," she said when she finally saw me. She rushed forward and hugged me tightly for the longest time. "You're all right. No one hurt you."

"I'm fine, Mom," I replied.

"I'm sorry about the intruder. I'm having a security system put in next week," Aunt Rose said apologetically.

"As long as you're both OK, that's all that matters," Mom replied. "I love you so much. I'll never leave you alone again. You're everything to me, and I couldn't handle if anything happened to you," she said as she continued to hold me tightly.

"I love you too, Mom, but I'm fine," I reassured her. I guess that she finally believed me because she released me and asked me about school. Aunt Rose helped Mom with her luggage, and they talked in the car on the way home. I felt a sense of peace when Aunt Rose finally pulled into the farm and I saw Susie in the pasture.

"Goodbye, Little Quack Quack," Aunt Rose said. "It was nice having you over."

"Bye, Aunt Rose," I replied as I dashed out of the car toward the barn. Susie ran up to me when she saw me, and I wrapped my arms around her neck as she nuzzled me with her nose. It felt like an eternity since I'd seen her instead of a few weeks.

"Lauren, I'm going to drive into town and get a few groceries. Would you like to come with me?" Mom asked.

"Is it OK if I just stay home?"

"Sure. I won't be long," she replied. I got Susie some oats and brushed her mane. I wanted to ride over to John's house and tell him about everything that had happened, but Mom would have been upset with me if I'd left without asking. I would see him at church tomorrow anyways. I put a saddle on Susie and rode around the pasture enjoying the beautiful day.

Mom arrived home an hour later and made sandwiches for dinner. They tasted like a gourmet meal in comparison to Aunt Rose's cooking.

"Did you have a nice time with Rose?" Mom asked as we ate our sandwiches.

"I guess so, except for the horrible food. I'm so happy to be home." I wanted to tell her all about Arabella and the other ghosts, but I promised Miss Peters that I would keep her secret. "Is it all right if I go to bed early?" I hadn't slept well in weeks.

"Of course. I just have a few dishes to wash. Goodnight, Pumpkin. Sweet dreams," Mom said as she kissed me on the forehead. I went upstairs and got ready for bed. I loved my bedroom with its faded floral wallpaper and lace curtains. I opened the window, and a cool breeze gently blew across my face. I snuggled under my covers, and for the first time in weeks, I slept with the lights off and dreamed of nothing.

"Lauren, wake up. We're going to be late for church," Mom called from downstairs. It felt like I had only fallen asleep a few minutes ago. I hurried to get ready and ran downstairs for breakfast. Mom had made scrambled eggs with bacon and toast. I wolfed down my entire plate in a few minutes, and we both rushed out the door. Mom handed me a bouquet of flowers to hold in the car. "I thought that we'd bring your dad some flowers today," Mom said with a hint of sadness in her voice. Once a month we visited his grave and placed some fresh flowers on it.

"I think that he'd like that," I replied. When we finally arrived at the church, the service had already started so we sat in the back. Mrs. Harrison could be heard snoring in one of the front pews. The readings were about having hope in the Lord and He would make your paths straight. Pastor Joe got up and gave his sermon.

"May our ripples of hope for each other and in God build a current that will carry us to a place of healing, love, and victory." I thought that by finding Arabella's birth mom, John and I had given her hope, and maybe that hope would bring her to a place of healing. Church finally ended, and I ran out toward the tables filled with donuts and coffee. John was waiting there and motioned for me to come over. His eyes were wide, and he looked upset.

"Lauren, be careful. The Donut Dictator is at the table. She's already yelled at me for trying to take more than one donut," he whispered. The Donut Dictator was an elderly woman who looked more like a prison guard. She must have seen me put all those donuts into my purse last Sunday and was policing the table today.

"You're only allowed one donut," she barked at me as I went up to the table.

"I know," I said as I had difficulty trying to pick only one donut.

"Lauren, which donut do you want?" Mom asked as she saw me struggling with my choice.

"I'm only allowed one, but I can't decide between the jelly donut and the apple fritter."

"Why don't you get the jelly donut and I'll get the apple fritter. Then you can have my donut," Mom generously offered.

"There is only one donut per person," the Donut Dictator commanded.

"Yes, I know, and I'm going to share my donut with my daughter. Is there a problem with sharing?" Mom asked. Pastor Joe sensed some tension and came over.

"Is everything all right?" he asked.

"I thought I'd share my donut with my daughter," Mom said pointedly as she glanced at the Donut Dictator.

"What a great idea. I'd like to share my donut with John. Why don't you pick another one out, John," Pastor Joe offered. John quickly ran to the table and picked out the chocolate donut that he had been eyeing. The Donut Dictator's face turned bright red, and it looked like her head was about to explode. John and I ran away with our donuts before a fight broke out and found a hidden bench to sit on.

"Guess what, John? I found Arabella's mother," I replied excitedly.

"It was your Aunt Rose, wasn't it?" he said confidently.

"No, it was Miss Peters," I announced.

"Wait, how it that possible? She wasn't even in his class," John said, confused.

"I know. They met when she was only a junior in high school. Her name is really Gladiolus, which is the name of a flower, but everyone calls her Gladys."

"I can't believe it," he said, astounded.

"I know. I couldn't believe it either. I gave her the phone number to the hospital that Arabella is staying at. She told me not to tell anyone, but I told her that you helped me find the adoption papers and the doll, so she said that it was OK if I told you. We're not supposed to tell anyone else."

"I won't," John promised.

"What are you two whispering about?" Mom asked.

"Nothing," I quickly replied.

"We should get going," Mom said.

"Bye, John. I'll see you at school tomorrow," I waved. John still looked shocked over the news. I felt the same way. Mom held my hand as we walked to the car. Once we got to the cemetery, we found my dad's grave.

"I miss you," Mom whispered as she placed the flowers in front of the tombstone. I saw someone in the distance and recognized Miss Peters.

"Mom, Miss Peters is here. Can I go over and say hi?" I asked.

"Sure. I'll meet you over there in a minute. I just want to pull some weeds and tidy up here," she said. I walked over to Miss Peters, and I could see that she was standing in front of Andrew Campbell's grave.

"Hi, Miss Peters."

"Hi, Lauren. I was just telling Andrew that you had found our daughter. I think that he would be happy about it. I called the hospital, and I've been given permission to visit her next weekend," she said as a worried look came across her face. "Do you think that she'll like me?" she asked.

"She's going to love you. I know that I do," I replied. Miss Peters turned and hugged me.

"Thank you, Lauren. Thank you for everything," she said. Mom came over and joined us.

"Hi, Gladys. Thanks for helping me out at the library while I was gone."

"You're so welcome. I've missed you, and it's great to have you back," Miss Peters replied. They talked for a few minutes, and I noticed a balding man in a track suit running at the park nearby. He waved at me and started to walk over. When he came closer, I realized that it was Melvin. I didn't recognize him without his fake hair.

"Hi, Lauren. It's nice to see you," he said.

"Hi, Mr. Melvin," I replied. I liked him. He had always been nice to me. "Mom, this is Mr. Melvin."

"Hello, I'm Elizabeth Evans," Mom said as she reached out to shake his hand.

"Nice to meet you. And this must be Lauren's older sister," Melvin replied as he smiled at Miss Peters. She giggled like a school girl.

"This is my friend, Gladys Peters. She works at the library with me," Mom replied.

"I'm honored to meet you," he said as he shook her hand. He seemed to hold her hand and smile at her for the longest time. Mom looked back and forth between the two.

"Lauren and I are going for ice cream. Would you two like to join us?" Mom asked. Mom had never said anything about ice cream, but I could never say no to food.

"I would love to come if Gladys would join us," Melvin asked expectantly.

"I didn't have any other plans," Miss Peters said.

"Then you'll come," Melvin said cheerfully. "Please take my arm. The ground is uneven here, and I wouldn't want you to trip."

"Thank you. What a gentleman you are," Miss Peters replied as she took his arm. Mom held my hand as we walked ahead of them toward the ice cream parlor on Main Street.

"Do you like cats?" I could hear Miss Peters ask Melvin.

"I do. I should probably confess that I have four of them myself. Do you like cats?" Melvin asked, hopeful.

"I love them," Miss Peters replied happily.

"Who knows, maybe there will be a wedding soon," Mom whispered in my ear. I looked back at Miss Peters and Melvin who were chatting away. I noticed a young blond man standing in the cemetery. He smiled at me, and I recognized the crooked grin from the yearbook pictures. It was Andrew Campbell. He waved at me, and I waved back before he disappeared into the sunlight.

"Who are you waving at, Lauren?" Mom asked as she looked back at the empty cemetery.

"No one," I replied.

"Look Lauren, there's a rainbow," Mom pointed to the sky. I looked up at the bright blue sky and could see a faint rainbow that seemed to end somewhere near the trees in the cemetery. "It's a heavenly day, isn't it?" Mom commented.

"Heavenly," I agreed.

Chapter 22

Six months later

I waited outside of school for John. Mom was getting out of work early today and offered to take John and me out to dinner. There was a thin blanket of snow that covered the ground, and I rubbed my hands together to keep warm.

"Are you ready?" John asked as he walked over to where I was standing.

"Yes. Did you find a restaurant that you wanted to go to?" I replied as we both headed toward the library where my mom was working.

"I wanted to try the new restaurant that opened up a few months ago. I looked it up online, and it got good reviews," John said eagerly. John liked food as much as I did, but his tastes where way more expensive than mine.

"I think that's the same restaurant that David Applebottom is the chef at," I replied.

"Is he still dating your Aunt Rose?" John asked skeptically.

"Yes, he is. Can you believe it? I think that's the longest Aunt Rose has ever dated anybody. I'm looking forward to trying his food." We had finally reached the library, and it was nice and warm inside. Miss Peters was sitting at the front desk. There was a beautiful bouquet of blue irises in a vase on top of her desk.

"Hi, Miss Peters. Those are really pretty flowers," I commented.

"Thank you. Melvin gave them to me. He said that they reminded him of the color of my eyes," she said as she smiled dreamily.

"How is Arabella?" I whispered, careful not to give away her secret.

"She is getting better and better every day. I talk to her every evening and drive down on the weekends to visit her. I'm petitioning the court to eventually get custody of her. I know that it will take some time, but I'm hopeful that she can come and live with me someday."

"That would be nice," I said.

"I almost forgot. Arabella wrote this letter to you two and asked me to give it to you." Miss Peters opened a drawer and took out an envelope and handed it to John who was standing nearby.

"Thanks," John replied.

"I should get back to work. Thank you both again for finding Arabella for me. I can't tell you how much it has meant to me," Miss Peters said as she hugged us both.

"You're welcome," I replied. John and I went upstairs and found an empty table in the back. John opened the envelope and took out the letter.

"What does it say?" I asked with both anticipation and fear. I didn't know what to expect. John began reading it out loud.

"It says, 'Dear John and Lauren...'"

"Wait." I interrupted. "Why did she put your name first?"

"Because I'm older," John replied.

"But I'm the one that she haunted," I argued.

"Do you want me to read it or not?" John asked, perturbed.

"Go ahead," I finally agreed.

"Here," John said as he placed the letter down on the table. "Why don't we read it together?"

"Thanks," I replied as I looked down at the handwritten note in front of me and started to read it.

Dear John and Lauren,

I wanted to thank you for finding my birth mother. I don't know how you did it, but you accomplished a miracle for me that I was starting to believe would never happen. I had often dreamt of a young girl and boy who were trying to help me, but I had only known pain and suffering in my life, and I could never believe that there was anyone out there who cared about me. I only knew how to lash out in anger and hate. Gladys was the first person in my life to show me what it was like to be truly loved. Her unending kindness and compassion have transformed me in ways that I didn't think were possible. I hope to see you both someday and thank you in person. I could never repay you for the blessing that you've given me, to be loved unconditionally.

Your friend,
Arabella

"That was really nice," I said as I wiped a tear from my eye. "We did it, John. We helped Arabella find her mom."

"Yes, we did," John said triumphantly. "Although I still think that there's a body buried in your aunt's backyard."

"No, there isn't!" I protested as I punched him in the arm.

"Owww! Well then who are we going to help next?" John asked as he rubbed his arm.

"I could use a vacation from ghosts for a while," I replied.

"We're both going to camp up in the mountains soon. I bet there are lots of ghosts there," John said enthusiastically.

"I hope not," I said, but you never know.

To be continued

The Hauntings in Montana Series

Made in the USA
San Bernardino, CA
16 August 2017